KIN
OF THE WORLD

BY
JASON BOJE

KIN OF THE WORLD

First Edition: November 2023

Self-Published by: Jason Boje

Cover Design by: Zaid Asghar

Interior Layout by: fiverr.com/malikmani007

For inquiries, please contact: jasontejiriboje@gmail.com

TABLE OF CONTENTS

US NOVATUS

"There used to be dozens of fantastical creatures in this space alone," stated Protector Aarush to the two young boys who stood to either side of him, both no older than a decade. "But those days are long behind us...."

With a swish of his caramel-coloured robe, Aarush gestured towards the bottom of the hill they stood on. The trio looked down at the decomposing mythical corpse, sprawled across the charred grass. Aarush closed his eyes and winced in pain at the tragedy. He conjured a ball of fire within the palm of his left hand to commemorate the creature.

The smaller, more energetic of the boys, Maximilian, stared at the dragon corpse with a face of wonder and awe. His mouth gaped open as his eyes glossed over its dark yet glassy charcoal scales. The taller, more composed of the two boys, Dillon, harboured a different reaction, one of outrage and disgust.

Maximilian looked into the creature's cold dead eyes, the excitement slowly seeping from his body. "But why?" he asked, pain rife through his cracking voice as he solemnly admired the dragon's scales. "Why would the Vyre do this?"

"Anything that harbours powers close to that of the True One's has to be eradicated as far as they're concerned," answered Aarush. He closed his fist, extinguishing the fire.

Aarush stared over the horizon, his wispy white beard moving through the wind. He took a deep breath, admiring the valley stretched out in front of them.

"Just like us novatus, right?" said Dillon, an air of uncertainty in his tone.

Aarush nodded at him slowly in agreement. "Just like us novatus."

The two boys looked up to Aarush, a melancholic look on his face. The already sour mood encapsulated amongst the three grew more and more sour.

"Follow me, boys," ordered Aarush, breaking the silence. "I have something else to show you...something worse."

Aarush slowly walked down the hill, gesturing at the two to follow him. The boys did so, but not without wary reluctance.

★★★

Moments later, the trio found themselves in the back of a horse-drawn carriage. They all wore their caramel robes with the hood up, partially concealing their identities as the driver of the carriage rode his horse through a poor dishevelled small town.

Maximilian hyperactively looked out of the window, excited at the sights the town had to offer. As they passed by a tavern, he saw a bloodied woman being dragged out of the bar by three men. The woman screamed in agony forming gusts of wind around her to try and aid her escape. To stop her, the men beat her into submission until her cries were no more.

"What the hell?" whispered Maximilian, gulping a heavy lump in his throat.

As they passed through the town centre, Maximilian saw a man in a metal cage. The man stood seven feet tall, yet was weak, malnourished, and dirty. Standing outside the cage were a group of townspeople who used spears to poke holes through the man's skin. The man yelped in pain breathing fire as he did so. The more painful fire he breathed out, the more his skin was sliced at by the townspeople.

Before Maximilian could even react to this, his attention was drawn elsewhere. They passed by an alleyway in which a group of criminals resided. The four criminals crouched over the dead body of a man with no eyeballs, in place of his eyes grew leaves and vines. The criminals butchered the man's body in an attempt to harvest his organs, pulling out the leaves and vines from each bloody crevice of the cadaver.

Maximilian covered his mouth in an attempt not to vomit, stricken with shock at all he had just witnessed, his body trembling. Aarush looked down at Maximilian. He saddened by the fact that the boy had to witness these sights yet did nothing to prevent him from doing so.

***

The carriage eventually took them to the middle of a dark, dreary, and heavily-vegetated forest. The three of them stepped off the carriage which rode away. Outside the forest, a large group of people could be seen, hundreds of men and women congregated together. The three novatus stood at the bottom of a monumentally sized rocky grass hill that led down to a slimmer, more daunting cliff edge.

"What are we doing? Where are we?" asked Maximilian, regaining his excitement and curiosity.

"You must be quieter, child," said Aarush. "It cannot be known that we are here."

Aarush instructed the boys towards the very end of the forest. They stopped by a set of large hanging tree leaves. From this position, they could see people on the cliff clearer. They saw that these people were split into three groups, with highly differing appearances.

The majority of the group consisted of fifty mainly upper-class citizens who stood a good distance away from the cliff's edge. In front of them and closer to the cliff's edge stood thirty black-cloaked guards who wielded long swords by their hips and stern looks on their faces. The last group of twenty people stood on the cliff's edge, all had their hands tied with rope and their eyes blindfolded by cloth. They looked to be beaten, bruised, and defeated, with a weak elemental aura surrounding them. Dillon's eyes widened with realisation.

"I know what's happening!" he whispered, tapping Maximillian on the shoulder violently. "That's the Vyre. And they're doing another novatus execution."

Maximilian's eyes widened similarly to Dillon's. The two boys darted their eyes towards Aarush for confirmation. He gave them a sad knowing nod.

"Oh no…" whispered Maximilian, directing his attention back to the cliff.

The twenty-nine other black-cloaked Vyre guards parted to make way for the leader, Nathanael Reyan, to walk through. A shiver danced its way down Aarush's spine as he saw the Vyre leader. He was a pale man whose mild-mannered appearance and slim stature did nothing to mitigate the air of dominance he carried with him.

Reyan walked with poise and dignity, carefully approaching the bound and blindfolded novatus by the cliff's edge. He double-checked that the rope that binds each of the novatus was tied sufficiently. Once sure that they are secure he turned to address the crowd of Vyre guards as well as the group of high-class nobles.

"Every man must come closer to God," Reyan affirmed. The crowd of people hung onto every word that came from his gravelly stoic voice. "But not too close."

Reyan drew his longsword, granting him a booming cheer from all of the nobles who came to observe. He turned one of the male novatus captives around. He faced the man and plunged his sword through them. The man let out a shocked gasp of deep quiet pain, blood leaking from his wound as well as his mouth.

"And whilst it's not your fault you were born this way," Reyan added. "It's not my place to deny God's will."

He then gently pushed them off of the cliff's edge and to their deaths. He repeated this process for each of the twenty novatus he came across. The gathered nobles chanted and jeered with such excitement and glee that one would think they were at a musical festival rather than an execution.

Maximilian struggled to stifle a tear as he watched dozens of his people being thrown to their deaths. Dillon, on the other hand, trembled with rage. He leapt up from his hiding place, urgently reaching underneath his robes. He retrieved a bow and a small quiver of arrows that he had hidden, taking out an arrow and placing it within the bow. Before he could even ready his shot, he was stopped by

Aarush, who placed his hands on Dillon's shoulder and shook his head in disapproval.

"Shouldn't we help them?" protested Dillon.

"No," answered Aarush bluntly. "You will soon see why."

Dillon resigned himself back to his hiding place, looking back toward the events on the cliff. Reyan continued the execution, the nobles continuing their chants of glory. With a gentle push of an elderly man off the cliff, there were only five novatus left. One of the remaining novatus shook her head in outrage. Though she could not see due to the blindfold, the sweat that beaded on her forehead was indicative of the sounds of her falling comrades taking a toll on her.

"I will not lay claim to your false God!" she screamed with defiance. She scrunched her face violently to the point where she almost popped a blood vessel. Using all the power she could muster, she managed to light a small fire with her fingertips. She burned the rope that tied her, freeing her hands which she used to tear the blindfold off her face.

Everyone who bore witness to this was surprised, to say the least, and outraged to say the most. Everyone but Reyan. She wasted no time running away from the cliff edge, desperate to make her escape. Reyan allowed her to leave, adding to the onlookers' shock.

The woman ran past the group of nobles who all clawed and grabbed at her in outrage, equally as desperate to see her executed.

With a calm raising of his hand, Reyan ordered the nobles to stop. The crowd slowly simmered down and allowed the girl to run away from them, fumbling her way up the hill. The nobles looked toward Reyan in confusion. He gestured at them to quieten down and wait.

The young woman raced up the hill aimlessly, panting as she sprinted with urgency. When she reached the top, she was faced with something that astonished her, striking fear through the very core of her body. Approaching her from the other side of the hill was a creature, who grew from a mere few inches to hundreds of feet tall by the time they were in front of her.

The godly creature possessed the muscular proportions of an otherworldly humanoid beast, the facial features of both a canine and a feline and the heaven-piercing horns of a mutated elk.

Both the nobles and the Vyre guards knelt in the presence of the creature, all captured in star-struck awe.

"Is that who I think it is?" asked Dillon, his throat gripped with fear.

"It is," answered Aarush.

Dillon and Maximillian hid themselves deeper within the leaves, frightened to no end.

"Welcome back, oh True One," greeted Reyan, bowing his lower.

The escapee remained glued to her position as she stood in front of the True One. Frozen in fear, the only part of her that moved was a weak trembling bottom lip. The godly beast glared at the woman; its black beady eyes filled to with untethered rage. Smoke emitted from its body as it breathes heavily, crouching down towards her.

"Please," whimpered the woman. "Spare me."

The True One scoffed at her pleas. It let out a beastly scream, loud enough to make the strongest of ears bleed. The scream harboured so much raw power that it continuously rang in the ears of everyone within its radius, including Aarush and the boys. Its most successful feat, however, was its instant killing of the young novatus woman. She dropped to the floor, her ears leaking and eyes filled with blood. The True One threw the woman's corpse into its mouth, swallowing her hole. With its first treat consumed, it stood back up and walked towards the cliff.

The nobles and guards frantically move out of the way, allowing the True One a direct route towards the edge of the cliff where Reyan and the remaining four captured novatus stood.

"Do with them as you please my Lord." offered Reyan, gesturing towards the final four.

The deity examined each of the four novatus. "Blasphemous creatures." it derided in a barely comprehensible growl.

The True One attacked the four in a fit of unrefined fury. It tore them apart limb by limb, dismembering them violently, and then consuming them in an equally horrific fashion.

This of all things, was what got the crowd to cheer and chanting. The nobles celebrated as their god desecrated the last of the novatus captives, crunching their bodies to a bloody paste within its sharp silver teeth.

Dillon and Maximilian watched on in speechless horror, their faces coloured by cold trauma. The two of them looked over to Aarush, stunned and confused as to why he brought them there. Protector Aarush closed his eyes and looked down to the floor, unable to face them.

"I'm sorry you had to witness that, boys. But it is for your own good." Aarush apologised. "It is not enough to hear of the horrors our people go through. You must live through them to gain a true understanding."

Once it had finished eating, the True One leapt over the cliff's edge and out of everyone's sight. The Vyre guards escorted the noble onlookers away from the cliff and up the hill, ready to resume their normal lives as if nothing happened.

Dillon shook his head in outrage, gripping one of his arrows in a tightly-closed fist. Filled with such fury, he snapped the arrow clean in half.

Maximilian clutched his stomach, feeling compelled to throw up once more. This time he was unable to stifle it, crumbling to his knees as he heaved up vomit. The young boy shook with such turmoil that lightning charged around his body. He dug his fingers into the muddy floors of the forest, crying and shaking as he muttered unintelligibly.

Protector Aarush crouched down to Maximilian, rubbing his back in a smooth, comforting motion. "Now do you see why we stay within the shelter?"

"Yes," Maximilian gasped in between tears. "I do."

Dillon helped him to get back up on his feet. Maximilian wiped his mouth clean, attempting to compose himself once more. Protector Aarush looked over the two boys, his arms connected within his robes, giving him a more noble look.

"I have a question for you boys," he said.

The boys looked up to see him staring attentively at them. His face was stern and stone-like, his sunken brown eyes seemed tearing straight through their souls.

"What is one to do when their very existence is condemned by a god?"

Maximilian and Dillon both stared at Aarush blankly, neither of them able to come up with an answer. Bewilderment was plastered across the two boys' faces as they racked their brains for one. Aarush chuckled, his demeanour softening.

"It's okay if you don't have an answer," he assured. "It's a question that has plagued us novatus since our conception, and one we still do not have a final answer for to this day."

The two boys looked at Aarush with engaged melancholic stares.

"But one day we will have that answer," assured Aarush defiantly.

His change in tone uplifted their moods ever so slightly. They looked up at him, still saddened and confused but with eyes of building hope.

"We will?" Maximilian asked.

"Of course, we will. We're a strong and noble people," stated Aarush. "The work you kids help the other protectors and I do at the shelter is what is going to lead us towards the day where we find that answer."

The two boys nodded in enthusiasm, taking in his words. Aarush directed their attention towards the glistening moon in the sky.

"Something tells me, that day is coming very soon."

The glimmer of hope in their eyes intensified, amplified by the sense of pride emanating from Aarush as he looked down at them with a smile.

MEMORIES OF GABRIEL

Hidden deep within a forest of tall robust trees was a large rudimentary abandoned building, formally a temple as grand as it was cream, but soon repurposed to house troubled novatus, young and old. The novatus, mostly children, teens, and young adults, wandered the grounds free and happy as if they had not a care in the world. Though it was easy to feel that way when Protector Aarush was watching over you. Aarush constantly surveyed the perimeter from deep within the forest, next to the temple. His eyes waned in vision, working to keep all the troubled young novatus within its gaze.

Standing far away from the temple, on the very edge of the forest was a particularly perturbed young novatus. Soft-faced, caramel skinned with short-dreaded hair and bright brown eyes, the boy looked the very picture of innocence as he stood at the forest edge with his fists clenched and body shaking. Though he seemed innocent and timid, the boy still gave off an essence of righteous bravado, jaw tensed and eyes fierce. This was the nature of Gabriel Elijah.

Gabriel was closely accompanied by two of his friends. Dillon Fachmann and Maximilian Abrego both children slightly older than him. The duo jokingly, and spitefully, dubbed 'Aarush's favourites' by the other children.

Gabriel looked over the dotted lines in the mud that signified the parameter of the shelter. He nervously attempted to step one foot over it but was ultimately too anxious to follow through. As he did so, Maximilian burst out laughing whilst Dillon shook his head.

"I knew you were too scared to do it, Gabriel!" Max chortled.

"Shut up Max!" Gabriel retorted, failing to hide the squeamishness on his face.

"Hey, you're the one who wanted to see what was out there!" Max laughed.

"I for one think it's best you didn't do it." Dillon sighed.

"Yeah, you're right." Gabriel accepted. "There's probably a good reason we're not allowed out there."

Dillon nodded in agreement; Max rolled his eyes. Seconds later, a loud ringing bell sounded in the background. Max tapped Dillon on the shoulder with the back of his knuckles.

"That's us bro, come on."

Gabriel watched on in frustration as the two started to stroll their way back to the shelter.

"Are you guys ever going to tell me where you go after that bell?" he asked. Max turned around briefly to smirk at him.

"There's probably a good reason you still don't know," he told him quietly.

Max turned again and headed back to the temple. Gabriel frowned as he watched them go. His gaze soon shifted away from them and looked up to a small glimmer of blue sky shrouded by the leaves of the tall trees that surrounded them. His eyes harboured both confusion and wonder.

***

Later that night, Gabriel lay on a fluffy cloth on the wooden floors of the room he shared with both Maximilian and Dillon. Unlike his roommates, he did not sleep well. Wide awake, he stared into space whilst he scratched a jagged birthmark on his shoulder blade.

As he scratched, Gabriel slowly noticed a strange twitching underneath the skin of his hands. Concerned, he sat up to inspect it.

He tried to hold it still but this only caused both hands to spasm. Gabriel worriedly panted as he inexplicably lost control of his hands. His eyes darted around the room and he began to notice a strange phenomenon - gusts of wind circling throughout the room. It wasn't long before Gabriel was in a state of hyperventilated panic.

Suddenly, a bolt of lightning struck its way through the ceiling above the room, landing an inch away from a startled Gabriel. The boy screamed, waking both roommates.

"Gabriel, what's wrong?" Dillon asked as he rubbed his eyes open. The lightning strike mark on the floor soon caught his eye.

"Oh…" Max gasped. He and Dillon shared a knowing look with each other, whilst Gabriel sat there still confused.

The bedroom door swung open, with Protector Aarush standing at the entrance, startling Gabriel to no end.

The old man rushed into the room with haste. The first thing he did was review both the lightning strike mark and the tremors of

Gabriel's hands. Gabriel slowly looked up at him in fear. He was surprised to see Aarush was not upset, but was smiling down at him.

"Come with me, boys."

***

Protector Aarush took the three boys into a giant room with golden walls. Inscribed on the walls were copious images of not just novatus but Vyre guards and The True One itself. At the top of the room, lined up against the walls were shelves of scrolls. Aarush reached for a scroll at the top of the shelf and slid it into the arm holes of his robes. Gabriel was astonished.

"Protector Aarush, what is this place?" he asked, "I've never seen it before."

"You never had a reason to," Aarush told him as he shut the door behind them. "Gabriel, I'm sure you have always wondered what this shelter was for. I'm sure you have wondered why we are all here and I'm sure you have wondered why we mustn't stray too far from the forest that surrounds us…"

Protector Aarush rubbed his fingers against his palms until a ball of light was generated from his hands. Gabriel gasped, taken aback, with Max and Dillon smirking at his reaction.

"It's because we…are novatus."

In unison, Protector Aarush, Dillon, and Max all revealed a small jagged glowing scar on their shoulder blades. Gabriel pulled down the collar of his shirt to see that the marks matched his birthmark exactly. The mark glowed a pale light he marvelled at it in wonder.

Aarush gestured at the three boys to sit down to which they obliged. Protector Aarush began to wield fire, using it as a storyboard. Using the fire as his imagery, Protector Aarush foretold the history of the True One and the novatus to Gabriel in its entirety as Max and Dillon listened in as if it was their first time hearing it too. From beginning to end, Gabriel's eyes widened and glossed over with awe. Aarush finished the story and extinguished the fire. For a while afterwards, Gabriel was speechless.

"Wow..." Gabriel gasped as he looked down at his hands. They trembled with fear as he gulped down a large lump in his throat.

"Remember Gabriel. Though the humans may consider us abominations and the creator of our world may see us as blasphemous creatures, it is *not* our fault that we possess such abilities," Protector Aarush told him. "At the very least, we can enjoy having them."

Protector Aarush smirked, nodding at Dillon who nodded back at him. Dillon walked over to the inscribed wall and pressed a hidden compartment which revealed a bow and a dozen arrows. Protector Aarush generated a ball of light on the wall opposite Dillon. From a distance, Dillon shot the arrows at a rapid-fire pace. Every single arrow hit the target surrounding the ball of light, each arrow evenly spaced from the other. Gabriel's mouth gaped open in surprise.

"Cool right?" Dillon chuckled.

"Whilst I am Kin of Sun, Dillon is Kin of Man," Aarush explained. "And within these shelters, us novatus can celebrate our differences unharmed."

"What about you Max? Which one are you?" Gabriel asked excitedly.

Max pointed his finger upwards wielding a small thundercloud.

"Kin of Skies. Just like you," he said.

Gabriel's smile stretched from ear to ear, eliciting laughter from the others.

***

The next morning, Gabriel stood in the shelter's park with Max and Dillon among many other novatus kids running around as they played games and experimented with their powers. Dillon carved a knife from wood whilst Maximilian played with the grass, bored as he could ever be. Gabriel looked at the trees above them, once again focusing on the small glimmers of blue sky that he could see beyond the leaves.

"Hey, Max. You know the way we are Kin of Skies?" Gabriel asked to which Max nodded. "Does that mean we can fly?"

A wry smirk planted itself upon Max's face. Without saying a word, he manipulated the wind below his feet, levitating with ease.

"No, I don't mean like that," Gabriel sighed. "I mean can we soar through the skies?"

"Soar?" chuckled Max. "That's a fancy word."

"You know what I mean. I want to soar. I want to soar high!" Gabriel told him, excitedly. "Come on, let's go fly further into the forest!"

"Sure." Maximilian shrugged. "You want to come to watch us fly, Dillon?"

Dillon shook his head. "No thanks."

"Suit yourself."

Maximilian bombed his way deeper into the forest, laughing all the way. Gabriel chuckled and followed him, clutching the chest of his racing heart.

***

The two eventually reached a spot within the forest with more space and fewer people. All of a sudden, Max shot up into the sky, flying high enough to reach the midsection of the incredibly tall trees. Gabriel watched in awe.

"Come on then, fly!" Max goaded him with a smirk.

Gabriel nervously started to hover over the ground, shaking profusely as he weakly built up the wind below him. Slowly but surely, he built up enough courage to fly on the same level as Maximilian and before they knew it, the two boys were ringing around the trees. The boys laughed and giggled as they flew in circles around each other.

Max looked like he could do this forever. But for Gabriel however, this lost its novelty rather quickly. He began to slow down after only a few minutes of their flying session.

"Oh, come on, don't tell me you're bored of flying already!" Max scoffed.

"I'm not bored, it's just that...I wish there was a way we could fly higher." Gabriel sighed. "Without all the tree leaves in the way."

"We can," said Max, that wry smirk returning.

That smirk of his had Gabriel immediately regretting making such a suggestion, hypothetical or otherwise. "Max, no. We mustn't-"

"I know, we mustn't stray too far from the forest. We'll just go slightly past it. That's not too far." suggested Max. Gabriel bit his lip in contemplation.

"Don't you want to soar?" Max goaded. Though he wanted to feign reluctance, Gabriel could not hide the excitement on his face.

Before he knew it, Gabriel and Maximilian were flying through the sky, a few metres away from the wooded forest. They had breached uncharted territory but neither cared, the freedom they felt at an all-time high. The pair perform flips and tricks as they soar through the sky together.

"WOO-HOO! YEAH!" Max screamed. The two boys let out laughs and screams of pure euphoria, the strong winds beating their faces and flowing through their hair. "You were right Gabe! This is epic!"

Gabriel giggled as Max flew around him. He looked at the uncluttered blue sky in all its beauty. "This...is the best day of my life," he celebrated as he let the wind take him in. Soon he was lost in the clouds of the sky, humming quietly as he soared with a calm serenity. Soon he was in heaven.

Distracted by the clouds in the sky, Gabriel was not privy to paying attention too much. And thus, he failed to see an archer shooting at him from the ground.

An arrow struck Gabriel, cutting the side of his body, and causing him to drop from the sky so fast it was as if he never belonged there. In a state of adrenaline and panic, Gabriel used his powers to create an air cloud, only barely cushioning his fall as he crashed to the ground. Maximilian continued to hover in the sky, looking down at him with concern.

"Oh, crap! Are you okay?" he asked.

The sound of another arrow swung through the air. In a matter of three brutal seconds, the arrows struck Maximilian through the head. With the bloody projectile pierced firmly through his temple, he plummeted to the floor with a sickening thud.

Gabriel's trembled, too shell-shocked to feel the wound that had been inflicted upon him or take his eyes off the wound that fatally struck Max. In just a few mere moments he was transported from heaven to hell.

With his arrow wound bandaged, a worn-faced Gabriel was joined by Protector Aarush as well as every single novatus from the wooden shelter of adult age. Together, they marched towards a stronghold on a grass field, daunting in size. The group all held the same look of intense anger and determination on their faces, apart from Gabriel. A few hours had passed since Gabriel saw Max die, but the look on his face held as if it had just happened.

"Can we please go back to the shelter?" Gabriel whimpered.

"No, we have to do this," Aarush insisted. "This isn't right."

When they reached the stronghold, Protector Aarush fists pounded furiously at the front door. It opened to reveal the leathery face of the disgruntled archer that shot Gabriel and killed Max.

"Oh great, more novatus," the archer scoffed. "Thought protecting this area was supposed to be easy work-"

With a fist full of light energy Aarush punched the archer hard in the face, effortlessly breaking his nose and buckling him to the ground. "How can you justify doing what you did to children?" he asked.

The archer glared up at him, spitting blood on the floor. "How can you justify breaching human territory?"

As if on cue a small army of archers and soldiers emerged from different areas of the stronghold castle front. Some came from higher floors, some from behind the building and some from inside backing up the main archer. The strong holders outnumbered the novatus shelter adults five to one. Despite this, Protector Aarush held his ground showing no fear.

The main archer attempted to finish the job, shooting an arrow at Gabriel. Protector Aarush knocked Gabriel out of the way and took the arrow to the chest. The attack barely phased him, only succeeding in angering him further. The two groups immediately devolved into bloody warfare against each other.

In a panicked dash, Gabriel crawled away to the safety of the nearest clump of raised grass he could find, his body shaking with anxiety. He watched on as the novatus fought with vigour, in spite of how quickly they were seeming to get overpowered.

"No, no, no…" Gabriel whimpered. His hyperventilation returned and his breath grew both heavier and weaker.

The young boy blacked in and out of consciousness as the fight progressed. He was confronted with the distressing sight of more and more of his people meeting a tragic end in the ongoing violence. The colour red flashed in his eyes as he witnessed the painting of a battlefield with novatus blood. He curled up into a ball and closed his eyes, hiding away deeper into the grass clump. A position he remained in for what felt like an eternity.

***

With his eyes closed he felt himself being picked up and carried away. Though he could not see he knew what was happening. He was being captured.

Gabriel kicked, screamed, and cried for mercy until… he started to feel himself flying.

He opened his eyes to see Protector Aarush carrying him with one hand and escaping to safety using fire to propel them with the other. He looked back down onto the battlefield to see that every other adult from the shelter had been ruthlessly killed, the archers making a mockery of their dead bodies in gruesome celebration.

Gabriel shut his eyes once more, tears streaming down his face. Aarush shook his head in sorrow, a single tear escaping from his eye as he flew on.

HEART OF A PROTECTOR

A decade had passed since Gabriel cried in the arms of Aarush as they fled the archers, traumatised for life. The people of the mainland of the First Kingdom were in much higher spirits, holding a celebratory parade for the Grand Leader and his royal family. Accompanying them was a legion of Vyre soldiers, led by an older and even more measured Nathanael Reyan.

Protector Aarush could also be found in the mainland of the First Kingdom at this point in time, though in a much worse state than Reyan. These days, a beaten-faced, worn-down, and barely-alive Protector Aarush could be found kept deep within a dark pit. He withered down there with his hands severely injured and enclosed within metal clamps.

***

A novatus shelter, grander than any other, occupied the land of a large and thin peninsula. The facility was made up of many different brick and stone-based buildings all scattered across the peninsula. Surrounding the main building of the shelter were some of the many novatus that resided there. Mostly young adults and adolescents, they spent their early mornings rigorously training with their Protectors. Visually, this facility was a vast improvement from the one the likes of Gabriel had grown up in a decade prior.

A much older Gabriel Elijah exercised on the polished wooden floors of his shelter room. He had grown into a muscular young adult with long dreadlocked hair yet still maintained his soft face. Gabriel did stomach crunches on the floor with such intense energy and determination that cyclones of wind formed around him.

Once Gabriel finished his exercise, he looked over a stone tablet calendar that lay underneath his bed.

"It's been over ten years since Aarush helped me move to this shelter," Gabriel sighed to himself as he noticed the date. "Isn't that ironic..."

***

Come afternoon time, the young adult Kin of Skies at the shelter practice drills together in an outdoor training ground. Each one used the wind to fly through a gruelling obstacle course constructed of wooden panels and platforms finishing off by striking a target with lightning. Though talented, every one of them made some sort of mistake whilst taking up this challenge. Everyone except for Gabriel. Gabriel completed his course, making zero errors and lightning-striking the target with perfect accuracy. The other Kin of Skies looked at Gabriel with faces of impressed admiration, especially the Protector overseeing the exercise. They gave him a round of applause upon completion. Gabriel smiled, equal parts bashful and prideful. This was what Gabriel saw to expect on a typical day at the shelter.

The training sessions concluded with each novatus returning to the grey stone buildings that made up their living quarters. As Gabriel left, he saw Dillon waiting for him, who had grown exceptionally tall over the years. The two greeted each other with a hug first and foremost.

"What are you doing now bro?" Dillon asked him as they walked back together.

"Probably going to do a joint training session with some of the Kin of Sun," Gabriel told him. "I reckon I could learn some techniques from them to supplement my own abilities."

Dillon rolled his eyes at this response.

"What?" Gabriel asked. "The rescue mission might be soon, remember."

"You won't be picked for the rescue mission if you die from exhaustion beforehand."

"Come on, you know how important it is to me," Gabriel said. Dillon nodded.

As the two continued to walk they passed by a group of people congregating around the entrance to the tall tents of the health building. They shared a troubled look and headed over to the crowd.

Gabriel and Dillon immersed themselves in the group to see what they were looking at. The people helped doctors in white cloaks usher in dozens of severely injured novatus refugees carried by their peers. One of the refugees wore a large thin open wound stretching from his cheek down to his ankle.

"Haven't seen injuries this bad since The Tragedy of the Wooded Shelter." one of the doctors commented. Like a flick of a switch, these words slowly sent Gabriel into a state of post-traumatic distress. His body tensed up violently as if he could still feel the arrows those archers shot him and Max with that haunting day. It took Dillon waving his hand in front of his eyes to snap him back to the present.

"You alright?" Dillon asked.

"Yeah, I'm just a little winded from training," Gabriel answered with a hoarse voice. He saw to immediately leave the area in a hurried stomp. Dillon watched him go, an unsatisfied scowl on his face.

***

That afternoon, a middle-aged, raven-haired Protector walked through the halls of the main building, her face buried in an important scroll she read attentively. She did not bother to look where she was going, her commanding presence being enough for most people to move out of her way. She ended up accidentally bumping into one person, however - Gabriel. He greeted her with a smile to which she groaned.

"Protector Bianca! It's good I bumped into you. I've been meaning to ask you about the intel progress concerning the rescue mission. I-"

"Everything is going according to plan and process Gabriel; I can assure you of that."

She tried to walk away but was stopped again by him much to her chagrin.

"I also wanted to ask about when the selection ceremony for the rescue mission is taking place. Soon I hope?" Gabriel continued to ask. "I've been training very diligently recently and want to make us-"

"For novatus sake Gabriel Elijah, will you calm down?" Bianca sighed. Gabriel lowered his energy, nodding. Bianca sighed as she looked down at him with sympathy.

"Look, I understand your enthusiasm. I know how much this means to you," she said. "But you need to relax. It'll get done. Stop worrying."

Protector Bianca walked to the side, this time managing to get away from Gabriel. He looked to the floor, shaking his head in disappointment.

***

Later, Gabriel stepped onto the stone arenas of the Kin of Sun training grounds behind one of the shelter's main buildings. He joined the trainees who engaged in light sparring matches with each other using their abilities.

One trainee seemed to catch his eye. The most active and bold of the novatus there. A young black man, six feet tall, slim yet toned, and with a face that was both welcoming in its handsomeness and intimidating in its scowled intensity. The infamous Kane Keahi.

Utilising a mixture of fire manipulation and martial arts throughout the session, Kane easily beat multiple opponents one after the other without taking a break or breaking a sweat. Gabriel watched all of his fights, looking equal parts impressed and envious. Once the sparring was done with, Kane returned the favour and started to watch Gabriel back.

"Hello, Gabriel," Kane greeted.

"Hello, Kane," Gabriel greeted back. Though the exchange was pleasant on the surface, Gabriel could not help but feel an intensity in the air when he locked eyes with Kane.

***

Hours after training and well into the evening time, every single young adult within the shelter was seated on polished logs within the cream stone enclosure of the ceremony room. Gabriel sat beside Dillon, eager to get it started. All the young novatus looked towards a stage in which all of the protectors stood, including Bianca. The silence that the room was initially held in was broken when she cleared her throat to speak.

"Today marks a year, six months, and fifteen days since the war officially ended," Bianca told the room of novatus. "And though the novatus lost to the humans, we can at least find solace in the relative peace our people have been afforded since its closure."

The protectors and trainees all nodded and murmured in agreement with her sentiments with some discussion coming up amongst those seated.

"Despite the level of death and destruction subsiding, we still suffer from the effects of said war," continued Bianca. "To this day dozens of our people remain prisoners of war at the mercy of humans. Including one of our most beloved Protectors, Aarush."

Utilising her Kin of Moon powers, Bianca created ice sculptures showing the audience each of those in need of rescue, one dozen ice structures of protectors and trainees alike, all lost to the war. Gabriel focused on the sculpture of Aarush in particular. His eyes watered, jaw clenched, and breath grew heavy. Dillon rested his hand on Gabriel's shoulder in an attempt to calm him down.

"But do not fear, for we plan to rectify this. As some of you may have heard, we are conducting a rescue mission for these prisoners," said the Protector.

With a turn of her nose, she gestured at one of the other protectors who joined her on the stage. The other protectors pressed hidden compartments in the walls behind them that revealed a series of fantastical stones with hollowed holes within them. The protectors showcased the stones to the on-looking crowd.

"We need three of you on the main mission itself and one of you involved with it, staying back here but keeping in contact with the others via mission stone," Bianca said as she gestured back to the stones. "Those selected will not only be greatly awarded upon completion but will be doing a great honour for our shelter and the novatus people as a whole."

The crowd of trainees bustled with excitement upon hearing this. Gabriel clenched his jaw even tighter. Protector Bianca nodded upwards with pride as she cleared her throat again.

"The first pick for the mission will be none other than...Magnolia Thorne."

A gorgeous white-haired young woman stood up from her seat with a beaming smile on her face. As the crowd gave her a round of applause, Magnolia used her Kin of Land powers to weave flowers into her hair giving her an even more glowing and beautiful image. Magnolia joined Protector Bianca on stage, bowing with grace then stood by her side.

"The second pick for the main mission is...Dillon Fachmann."

Dillon stoically nodded as the crowd gave him a round of applause. Gabriel looked at him with a face filled with surprise. Dillon smirked.

"You're not the only one who trains hard."

Gabriel watched in awe as Dillon joined Magnolia on stage, eager to join them.

"And my third and last pick for the main mission is..." Protector Bianca started, building increasing anticipation amongst the students. Gabriel clenched his jaw even tighter to the point where he almost shattered his teeth.

"...Kane Keahi." Bianca finally said.

As he stood up, Kane was given a larger round of applause than Magnolia and Dillon combined. He walked upon the stage, a face of smug satisfaction. He looked immensely pleased with his selection, unlike Gabriel who was livid.

"Which makes the final pick and mission stone holder...Gabriel Elijah." Protector Bianca finished.

"No, this can't be..." Gabriel grumbled under his breath.

Though Gabriel was given a round of applause, he was too upset to appreciate or even acknowledge it. He reluctantly stood up to join the other three on stage.

"This can't be..." he muttered, staring at the floor as he marched his way onto it.

"These are the four brave novatus who will free our-"

"THIS CAN'T BE!" Gabriel blurted out, interrupting the protector with a desperate shout.

His outburst sent the room into a state of awkward silence as he continued to lose composure. Bianca glared at him.

"What is your problem?" she sighed as she looked down at him.

"You don't understand...I need to be on the main mission, I-"

Irritated as ever, Bianca grabbed Gabriel, pulling him off of the stage and taking him aside.

"Why are you behaving this way?" she asked in an angered whisper.

"Please Protector Bianca, I *need* to be on the main mission," Gabriel begged. "You must understand that...I need to make this right."

Bianca pinched the bridge of her nose in frustration, letting out a sigh. She placed both hands on Gabriel's shoulders and looked him deep in the eyes.

"Please don't get the wrong idea, Gabriel," Bianca told him with a soft voice. "You are more than skilled enough to undertake the main mission; in fact, you were the first I had in mind. It's just...your relationship with Aarush makes me reluctant to put you forward."

"But what about Dillon?!" Gabriel protested. "He was originally from the same shelter as Aarush and me!"

"It's different with you," Bianca sighed. "You know this."

Gabriel's head slowly lowered in defeat. He knew she had a point. He knew she was right. As Bianca looked into Gabriel's sad eyes, she felt a hand placed on her shoulder. She turned to see it was Kane who had an odd look on his face as if he was attempting to stifle a smirk.

"I'll swap places with him," he said, much to the surprise of everyone in the room, especially Gabriel.

"Really?" he asked.

"Yeah, if you're willing to fight for it," Kane told him. "I challenge you to a Novaldem."

The crowd of trainees oohed and ahhed as Kane's intense gaze lasered in on Gabriel. It had been a while since any two trainees had engaged in a Novaldem other than light sparring, it was a rare occurrence, even in this situation. Before he answered Kane, Gabriel looked to Bianca for approval. Though she seemed immensely reluctant she slowly nodded her head.

"Very well," she accepted. The crowd chanted and jeered loud uproarious glory as Kane and Gabriel stared each other down.

"Oh no…" Dillon sighed, shaking his head as he watched the two.

Whilst Gabriel looked stern and determined, Kane seemed excited, almost lustful at the prospect of their upcoming fight.

NOVALDEM

All the novatus trainees and protectors who were gathered within the ceremony enclosure had gathered outside on the facility in the dead of night. They stood in a circle around a rough patch of grass surrounded by torches to light the area. Within the green were Gabriel and Kane, facing each other with menace.

A young Kin of Beast trainee morphed into a bear and let out the loudest of roars, signalling the beginning of the Novadlem.

Gabriel and Kane ran towards each other as the crowd cheered them on. Gabriel brought on the first attack of the fight, directing a bolt of lightning to which Kane expertly double-flipped out of the way. The crowd adored the move. Gabriel did not.

He continued his campaign of attacking, sending multiple gusts of wind Kane's way. Kane dodged every one of these blows. He retaliated by forming a wall of light energy, using it to temporarily blind Gabriel. Gabriel waved aimlessly, unable to see. Emerging from the light came Kane with a fist full of fire which he used to diving-punch Gabriel to the ground.

Gabriel quickly picked himself up from the floor just in time to evade a series of fireballs Kane blasted his way. He shot an especially large fireball in Gabriel's direction, but Gabriel used the wind to redirect it towards Kane. Before it could hit him, Kane used a roundhouse kick to slice clean through the fireball. The crowd roared once more to which Kane basked in the glory.

Gabriel used this distraction as an opening to charge at Kane with a surprise attack of lightning bolts as he flew towards him. Kane redirected every bolt with shots of fire as he closed the distance between the two. He shot more fireballs towards Gabriel until he was close enough to grab him. Despite his efforts to stop him, Kane grabbed Gabriel by the neck. He threw Gabriel down and then pinned him to the ground as he stared deep into his eyes. Gabriel saw that look of lustful excitement within his eyes again as Kane constricted him to the point he could barely breathe. Gabriel saw the match slipping away from him, as well as his life. He struggled and struggled, yet it was to be of no use.

But all of a sudden, Kane's grip on his neck weakened, the look from his eyes dissipating into that of boredom. Though initially confused, Gabriel immediately took advantage. He used it as an opportunity to reverse the grapple and eventually pinned Kane to the ground. As he did so he noticed Kane made no efforts to struggle against it. After a few seconds of Gabriel effortlessly pinning Kane, the Kin of Beast officiator roared once more signalling the end of the fight and subsequently, Gabriel's swift victory.

"I guess that settles it!" announced Protector Bianca. "Gabriel will take Kane's place on the main rescue mission!"

The cheers and roars that the crowd had previously reserved for Kane were now being wildly brought out for Gabriel. Gabriel looked around in honour as he saw the people of the shelter celebrate him. Even Kane seemed humble in defeat.

Dillon and Magnolia rushed over to congratulate him.

"Well done man!" Dillon celebrated as he patted Gabriel on the back.

"Thank you," Gabriel chuckled, sighing with relief.

"I think we know who our mission leader's going to be!" Magnolia beamed at him. Gabriel smiled as he stared back into Magnolia's captivating blue eyes. He was not completely familiar with Magnolia and this was only the third time he could remember them ever talking to each other. Up until now, Gabriel had only admired Magnolia from afar, so it took him aback to see her lump such high praise on him.

"Thanks, Magnolia." he graciously responded.

Gabriel let out another sigh of relief that turned into a quiet chuckle as he muttered to himself. "Don't worry Aarush. I'm coming to save you."

He stood in one place as the crowd of trainees and protectors dispersed and headed back to their sleeping quarters.

Kane however, walked in the darkness on his own, heading past the pond and towards the forest. The complete opposite direction to where the others were going. Gabriel jogged to catch up with him.

"Hey man, good match," he said, offering Kane a handshake. Though sceptical, Kane graciously accepted the handshake and even pulled him in for a hug. This surprised Gabriel, to say the least, but he quickly accepted his embrace.

"You're welcome…" Kane whispered into Gabriel's ear. "…for the act of charity."

"Sorry, what?" Gabriel asked in confusion. Kane heated the hand that was placed on Gabriel's back. Feeling the burn, Gabriel hastily pushed Kane off of him. He twisted his neck to the side to see Kane had burned a hole through the back of tunic shirt. He looked back to see Kane's malevolently smirking face.

"What the hell is wrong with you?!" Gabriel exclaimed. "And what do you mean by charity?"

"Don't be so goddamn stupid." Kane snapped at him. "Did you honestly think that you won that fight fairly? What, did you think me loosening my grip and then allowing you to pin me was just your skills pulling through?"

"Are you serious?" asked Gabriel, a scowl worn on his face.

"Deadly," Kane grunted.

Gabriel glared at Kane, silent with disbelief. Kane clenched his fists, smirking back at him.

"Now that we have that cleared up, I need you to remember two things. One: as I have practically given you one of the main positions on the rescue mission, you are now indebted to me." he lectured as he menacingly approached Gabriel. "And two: you will never, *ever*, be better than me."

Kane patted Gabriel on the shoulder aggressively. He slipped past him and continued his walk past the pond. Gabriel stood there in disbelief, unsure of how to process the situation. He resolved to just shake his head and leave it be, walking in the opposite direction Kane as he returned to his sleeping quarters.

***

Elsewhere, miles away from the shelter, the peninsula and all their ongoings, Nathanael Reyan was deep within the outskirts of the First

Kingdom. Using a staff, he managed to climb up and reach the second-most tier of a layered mountain and enter the cave situated adjacent to it with ease. Though gruelling for most, the journey was not even as much as a mild inconvenience to him. He would take multiple trips twice as gruelling if it meant seeing his god again. Once he entered the cave, he cleared his throat to speak, the sounds echoing off of its walls.

"True One my lord...you will be pleased to know that-"

Nathanael Reyan's face almost melted down and turned to stone as his eyes met the back of the cave. As he looked further, what he saw horrified him completely.

The True One was not only incredibly ill and suffering - they were near death.

THE PRINCESS AND THE FLOG

Of the Four Kingdoms of the Known World, the Third Kingdom was by far the most extravagant. Regular parades were hosted throughout the land to celebrate even the most inane of events. From the third month of regular clean water in a row to the celebrations of the prince's cousin's daughter's first birthday, any excuse to celebrate and the Third Kingdom would take it. Royalty, aristocracy, middle-folk, peasants, bannerman, Vyre soldiers, drum bands, and various amounts of horseback riders would often gather within the mainland, just outside the imposing green-covered castle of Grand Leader Roosevelt Thorne of the Third Kingdom.

These celebrations, however, were not always of a positive nature. It was often joked that the worst fate for a citizen of the Third Kingdom was to be involved in a public shaming in the square outside the grand castle. Though for some people, on some days, it was not a joke but a reality. And one of those people was none other than Magnolia Thorne.

The memory of that fateful day constantly returned to Magnolia. It breached her mind whilst she went through the day and filled her dreams as she tried to sleep through the night. Though it would never go through the full scale of events. She would always only recall glimpses - the sound of the crowds booing, the sight of the Vyre soldiers marching, and the taste of blood in her mouth...

Admittedly, Magnolia was glad the memories came back to her that way. She did not know if she could ever go through that full day again, mentally, or otherwise.

Thankfully, Magnolia's next day was not as filled with terror as those dreams had made her the previous night. After making her hair and skin look as prim and pristine as they possibly could be, she left her cabin in the hopes of starting a day as perfect as she was.

First and foremost, she decided to spend her morning with the youth of the cabins by the lake. They were a group of very young Kin of Land trainees, mostly pre-teen girls who adored and looked up to her. Magnolia could spend the whole day braiding their hair and listening to their stories, but as midday approached, it meant she would have to attend to other duties.

Magnolia was one of the few trainees who bothered to lend a helping hand to the kitchen and cleaning staff regularly. She loved the staff women, for they would always call her "Magnolia-Dearie." She hated the staff men though. They would either make crude remarks or call her names. Like 'human apologist,' for reasons that were obvious to most given Magnolia's past, though she would pretend she had no idea what they were talking about.

Later in the afternoon, Magnolia joined the likes of Dillon and Gabriel in one of the outdoor decorated, indoor training rooms for the most important part of all of their days - mission training. The trio worked around the clock in preparation for the rescue mission. Today, training consisted of navigating their way through the rooms as the Protectors used their powers to generate training dummies constructed of fire, ice, earth, and lightning that would become sentient and attack the trainees. Their goal was to make their way through the area untouched, whether it be through attacking or evading.

Gabriel summoned his control over wind and air to swiftly dodge out of the way of the attacking dummies. Dillon used his Kin of Man abilities to expertly dispatch the constructed enemies with a sword and shield. Magnolia used her Kin of Land abilities to do both. She not only completed the task but sought to show off whilst doing so. In an ingenious manoeuvre, she had utilised her Kin of Land abilities to generate strong mud vines from underneath the surface and use them as both florae stepping stones to get around the dummies that would immediately grow outwards and attack any dummy that attempted to pull her off the vine. Through this tactic, Magnolia ended up being the first to complete the task by a considerable margin. She immediately looked towards all of the Protectors, who stood on stone away from the grass training fields. They looked pleased with her and she looked pleased they were.

"Fantastic as always, Magnolia!" congratulated Protector Bianca once the day's sessions were over and the trio was wiping the sweat from their brows.

"As always," Magnolia repeated, beaming to herself happily as she rubbed her neck with a towel."

"Well done to all of you three. If you continue this great work, we can start the first set of official missions very soon." Bianca told the trio. "In the meantime, you boys better keep up.

Magnolia gleefully smiled at Dillon and Gabriel, both of whom scowled back at her, looking a touch jealous.

"Speaking of boys, I've not seen Kane Keahi down here in about a week," commented Protector Bianca. "Have any of you seen him?"

She was met with no answer. The Protectors' eyes scoured over the three of them. Magnolia shrugged, Dillon had nothing but a blank expression on his face and Gabriel looked as if he wanted to say something but could not.

"Great." Bianca scoffed. With a wave of her hand, she dismissed the trio, sending them away as she returned to discussing with the other Protectors.

"Hey, you want to do something this evening?" Dillon asked Gabriel.

"I'm already doing something this evening," Gabriel told him.

"Let me guess, more extra training?" asked Dillon. "Lord, do you ever do anything else?"

"Last time I checked, the Protector that damn near raised us is still being kept in a pit by the humans and it's up to us to save him." Gabriel snapped back at him. "So, you can damn forgive me for not being able to think of much else."

Gabriel shook his head and walked off in annoyance. Dillon sighed, his usual nonchalance gone, wishing he had not said anything.

"He has a point." Magnolia chimed in. Dillon rolled his eyes at her. She shrugged and left the training room too.

***

Tired from the day's training, Magnolia was quick to get an early night, relegating herself to her sleeping quarters by the early evening.

With decorative pink leaves lining the walls, a plush moss carpet laid over the wooden logs of the floor, and a fluffy white duvet of sewn-together feathers, Magnolia's was one of the much nicer rooms at the Novatus Protection Shelter. So, it would be no surprise that someone would be able to get so comfortable there. Yet Magnolia struggled to stay that way, nonetheless.

Wide awake and unable to sleep, her mind was too focused on the prospect of the mission. Though she did well in training she could not help but feel cripplingly anxious. Any moment the three of them could be asked to finally breach into the human territories of the First Kingdom, to retrieve those they had just lost. How nervous Gabriel seemed alone was enough to shake her. He was always so concerned about saving a "Protector Aarush" in particular. When she had asked him why, all he told her was that he had to 'rectify a mistake,' which did not make it any clearer and only seemed to fuel her anxiety. At times, Magnolia wished that Kane had remained the mission leader. Despite all the stuff she had heard about *him* in particular.

When Magnolia fell asleep, she found herself in a dream world once again. But this time she did not suffer the memories of that awful 'celebration day,' instead, her mind delved back to the exact day before it.

"Please Esra! Please! Get him to change his mind!" a younger Magnolia cried as she begged at the feet of a maid in the dark barely lit hallways of the Thorne Palaces.

"I can do no such thing," Esra told her, sounding mostly nonchalant and only the slightest bit sympathetic.

"Esra…you can't let them do this to me!" Magnolia cried.

"It's out of my hands…" Esra sighed. "I-"

Magnolia was yanked out of her dream and back into reality. She woke up to hear blood-curdling screams coming from both the building she was in, but across the shelter and peninsula as a whole. Magnolia immediately darted towards the other end of her room, where fluffy blinds covered a hole in the wall surrounded by a wreath forming a window. She looked out to see that every building, every field, and every training ground within the shelter's compounds was being attacked and ransacked by a group of armed soldiers. Not just any soldiers, but the Vyre itself.

Magnolia rushed outside to witness countless Vyre soldiers chasing novatus out of their sleeping quarters with brandished swords, sprinting around the compound either cutting down or capturing as many as they could. Magnolia thanked her lucky stars that despite how much her quarter-mates screamed in terror, the Vyre had not seen to come to her side of the compound yet. That meant she had time to try and process the situation and how she was to deal with it.

As Magnolia thought to herself, she saw a bolt of lightning shoot down from the sky in the distance. She looked across the peninsula to see it was being struck from behind the main building of the shelter. She recognised that jagged blue lightning, it was certainly not naturally occurring, she had seen it in training quite a few times before. That must be where Gabriel and the others were, she thought. Meaning that must be where she should be.

Using her vines to travel through the sky, Magnolia struggled to make her way through the quickly building chaos that was becoming of the peninsula, with novatus and Vyre soldiers engaged in gruelling fights of elements and blades. Dodging and weaving as she glided via vines, Magnolia barely avoided becoming the victim of collateral damage numerous times as she moved her way from her building to behind the main one. When she finally arrived at her destination, it seemed even more danger was waiting for her.

As expected, Magnolia arrived to see thirty of the most powerful novatus protectors and trainees clumped together, including the likes of Protector Bianca, Gabriel, and Dillon. Magnolia immediately blended in amongst this crowd. All of them were sweaty and panting like they had just spent their time tirelessly defending something. And looking at what stood across from them it was clear to see why. A much larger crowd faced them - Hundreds of The Vyre. A legion led by Nathanael Reyan himself...

Magnolia could not believe her eyes. It took all the strength in her body for her not to crumble to the floor from anxiety and shock. What on Earth had she just stumbled upon?

"What is the meaning of this Reyan?! How can you be so quick to forget the post-war agreement?!" Bianca panted. "We novatus have not breached your territory, how dare you breach ours?!"

"You novatus have not breached our territory *yet*," Reyan corrected her. "I don't think I'm mistaken in assuming that sooner or later, you would have come to take back your prisoners of war."

"We had no such plans," Bianca lied brazenly.

"Of course," Reyan scoffed. "Well whether you did or not hardly matters anymore..."

Reyan made a sideways nodding gesture to some of the soldiers that surrounded him. From behind him a series of Vyre soldiers scrambled in a group to retrieve something. Moments later, the decapitated head of a prisoner of war passed amongst the laughing men until it reached Reyan. Reyan immediately dropped the head to the floor in disgust. He kicked it towards the novatus' as if he was passing them a football.

"You can have this one back," Reyan told them. "He was my least favourite."

Bianca and the others looked down at the corpse head that was returned to them. Upon first glance, it was hard to tell who the head belonged to due to how much the face had been mangled. But upon further inspection, it became clear to all who it was.

"Oh, my Lord," Bianca gasped as she looked down at the head of the deceased Protector Aarush. Magnolia's eyes immediately darted toward Dillon and Gabriel. Dillon's lip trembled as his body shook. Gabriel on the other hand did not move a muscle, like he had been turned to stone. His eyes were widened and still. At that moment her heart broke for him.

"Are you trying to start another war?" Bianca asked, her voice trembling with anger.

"War?" Reyan scoffed. "No...there are much more matters at hand,"

Reyan unsheathed a vanta-black longsword from his scabbard. Frosty ice built up within Bianca's clenched fists. Both groups followed their leaders' actions. Before Magnolia could even blink, the two groups were racing to engage each other in battle once more. Vyre Soldiers versus Shelter Protectors. Humans versus Novatus.

***

The fight between clans took enough but a few minutes to turn into a gory mess of violent hatred. With flashes of fire, water, darkness, light, earth, lightning, and air, every novatus made sure to utilise their powers to the best of their abilities in attacks of raw energy. Though these efforts seemed almost futile as for every single novatus fighting, there were four humans fighting back. Most struggled to hold their own in battle, even Magnolia, who for every earth or plant-based attack she could execute against one opponent, she would have to reel back to avoid being cut to pieces by the other three. Only two novatus seemed to be holding their own relatively well in battle.

The first was Gabriel who fought like an efficient machine, slicing through Vyre with lightning and air. Though he fought like a man filled with ferocious fury, he looked like one who was dead inside. The second was Protector Bianca, though she had no other choice, as she was going up against Reyan himself.

Magnolia had heard of human swordsmen powerful and skilled enough to take on the elemental capabilities of novatus, but this was ridiculous. When Bianca attacked him with an ice wall, he effortlessly cut it in half like he was carving through a soft cake. When Bianca rained sharp icicles down on his head, he deflected each every single one. When Bianca attempted to freeze the ground beneath him, he jumped away from the ice floor and lunged in, closing the distance to her. Reyan engaged Bianca in direct combat, swinging his sword at her continuously, forcing her to track back as she blocked the blows by coating her arms with ice. Reyan remained undeterred by her defences, closing the gap between them with every strike.

Eventually, Reyan's attacks proved to be too swift and foreboding and Bianca's abilities were unable to keep up. The next set of slashes from Nathanael Reyan's cut through her skin and cut deep. Soon the Protector was on her knees, her forearms bloodied and midriff opened.

"Protector Bianca!" Magnolia exclaimed in fear as she saw this unfold. This was a mistake. Distracted from her fights at hand, one of the Vyre saw an opening to stab her in the back. To mitigate the brunt of the blow, Magnolia generated an earth wall behind her. But courtesy of her lack of attention she miscalculated the application of her abilities. Thus, not only did the blade still manage to graze her, but she accidentally generated the Earth wall right underneath her feet. The earth wall erupted upwards, sending her flying dozens of feet away from the battlefield, soaring and screaming across the pond. Magnolia's body landed near the other side of the peninsula, immediately knocking her unconscious on impact.

***

Magnolia woke up an unspecified amount of time later, painfully picking herself up from the charred grassy floor below her. After levying a series of disparaging curses against herself under her breath, she got up to venture back to the battlefield. As Magnolia walked through the peninsula, she pieced together what had happened during her absence. The areas that were once filled with ransacking Vyre and fleeing novatus were empty. Buildings had been burnt down, grass fields had been charred out and she could not walk three steps without seeing a dead novatus body. When she finally reached behind the main building again, the sights only became worse. She saw that the battle had ended, and Reyan and the Vyre legion had left a massacre in their wake. Of the thirty protectors and high-level trainees that she had seen come to the battle, only six remained breathing.

One of these few was Protector Bianca who suffered from a gashed cut from her left eyeball down to her midsection. The Protector was cut to pieces and practically comatose. Two of the other surviving novatus, a protector and a trainee, attempted to tend to her and her wounds, though it was clear to all there that she would not be waking up anytime soon.

"No way…no fucking way!" Magnolia cried as she saw the pitiful state of affairs. She scanned the field of littered dead bodies to find anyone else that she recognised that was still standing. She found no such luck until…she saw Gabriel on his own at the very end of the battlefield, kneeling on his knees as he stared at the floor. With tears flowing down her face, Magnolia sprinted towards Gabriel.

"Gabriel! I'm so glad you're okay!" Magnolia gasped as she crouched down to hug Gabriel from behind. "How could we have lost so badly? What happened here?!"

"Reyan happened," Gabriel told her with a quiet sombre voice. His head tilted down, tilted downward on something, refusing to turn around.

"Where's Dillon, is he alright?" asked Magnolia. Gabriel still did not turn around. With a backwards nod he gestured to the battlefield behind them. Instantaneously Magnolia spun around and looked through the row of corpses to find Dillon. She saw him at the middle centre of the field, with his signature blade protruding from his sliced-open forehead.

"Oh, my Lord…" Magnolia gasped. "Gabriel are you okay-"

Magnolia moved around Gabriel so she could look him in the eye. She saw what he was refusing to turn around for or take his eyes off of.

Sat in Gabriel's lap was Protector Aarush's head, to which he cradled dearly. Magnolia let out a dejected sigh. Filled with both tears and blood, Gabriel's tired and worn eyes finally looked up from the head and contacted Magnolia.

"This has to stop." Gabriel cried softly. "This has to stop…"

***

That midnight, Nathanael Reyan made the journey up the Holy Mountain once more, though, on this occasion, he was not alone. He was accompanied by a dozen Vyre soldiers all carrying the captured, unconscious, and even dead bodies of the novatus from the shelter with them into the large mountain crevice. Waiting for them at the end of the cave was The True One. The godly creature was just as sickly as Reyan had last seen it, its golden fur growing paler and heaven-piercing horns starting to turn downwards. Upon Reyan's orders, the Vyre soldiers dumped the novatus bodies they collected in front of The True One. Then, they waited.

After a few minutes, The True One awakened. Without hesitation, the first act the creature committed upon leaving their slumber was to devour the bodies of the novatus that were laid in front of them. In a matter of seconds, The True One had made a bloody fleshy mess of the meal and finished it whole. With the novatus consumed, it received instantaneous improvements in health, its fur growing slightly and horns turning upwards. The creature grunted with pleasure.

"More…" The True One ordered Reyan. "More…fresh…"

"As you wish," Reyan said with a bow.

THE BREW
OF TRANQUILLITY

Gabriel had been born into this world not just as a novatus but as an orphaned novatus. He considered himself lucky, for if it was not for Protector Aarush taking him into the first shelter, he would have been killed on the streets. And if it was not for Maximilian and Dillon, he would have grown up lonely within said shelter with no family and no friends. But thanks to those three, he received a sliver of a chance in life. Now all three were dead, and never in his life, had Gabriel felt lonelier.

That morning was supposed to be the day in which Gabriel, Dillon, and Magnolia embarked on their first try at the rescue mission for the prisoners of war. But considering recent events, it was clear it was no longer the case and that it never would be. That morning was instead spent like the last few mornings were, picking up the pieces after Reyan's attack.

With most of the protectors having been either killed or captured by Reyan and The Vyre and most of the surviving trainees shellshocked, the entire Novatus Protection Peninsula Centre was a catatonic mess. Gabriel spent the morning cleaning up blood from the facilities, clearing out bodies, helping with the rebuilding plans, and tending to those who were gravely injured, all tasks that made him even more depressed about their current situation.

These processes were slow in the wake of the absence of Protector Bianca who still lay in a hospital bed, alive yet unresponsive. Due to this, as a whole, the surviving higher-ups of the centre were not feeling very confident about the future. Gabriel had even overheard them discussing the prospect of scrapping the Peninsula Centre entirely and relocating most of the novatus here to the hidden shelters in other Kingdoms. The notion of a novatus finding a shelter to stay safely in when even the Peninsula which was considered the premiere shelter got attacked, was a ridiculous one. So, the fact that the higher-ups were considering it only confirmed what Gabriel had thought. The situation was bleak, dire, and not to improve anytime soon.

Gabriel was not one to give up, however. Like he had told Magnolia after they lost the battle, this had to end.

***

"Have you heard the news?" asked one young man to another. Both guarded an important stone-doored room within the main building, though in a lackadaisical manner. "The True One is ill again…"

"So?" asked the other man two.

"So? So, the last time that beast got ill, I he secreted a lot more energy into the ground." explained man one.

"So?" asked man two again.

"So that means many more novatus are going to be born at random again, stupid!"

"What? That's a load of bull."

"It's not! That's why Reyan captured so many when he attacked. He's feeding them to The True One so it can stop being sick and secreting all over!" explained man one.

"What? Really? Man, am I glad I'm not one of those who got caught." said man two.

"Don't hold your breath." said man one. "I don't think it's long until the humans come back for the rest of us."

"Aw, crap."

"Crap indeed."

A few minutes after their conversation had passed, the two guards walked away from the door to embark on their break. Gabriel emerged from his hidden eavesdropping position around the corner from. With a determined sigh, he marched his way to the stone door. From the hesitance in his face and tightening of his jaw, it was evident that Gabriel thought he had no business entering this room. But he did so anyway. Gabriel constructed a ball of air and placed it inside the keyhole lock of the door. With immense amounts of power, Gabriel constricted and expanded the air ball until the padlock exploded.

He opened the door and was met with a vast room that looked even larger on the inside. The room acted like an empty stone passageway with not much in terms of furniture. The real contents of the room were on either side of the walls. Stone shelves with thousands upon thousands of scrolls were neatly organised amongst these hundreds of shelves. It all reminded him of the same room Aarush had told him he was a novatus, the night his powers had first developed.

Gabriel was amazed by the sheer amount of information that was available to him, having no clue where to even start. Gabriel generated a powerful air wall and used it to block and lock the door behind him. He mindlessly picked the first scroll he found off of a stone shelf and got to reading.

***

After spending hours within that room and pouring through almost fifty scrolls, Gabriel had learnt a lot about the novatus' place in the world. He learnt interesting facts such as how only one in every one-thousand people was likely to be born with novatus abilities. He also learnt interesting theories on the True One's origin, most of which theorise him to be an otherworldly creature from a species of creatures who only have the compulsions to create, destroy and consume. Gabriel could only wonder if any of that was true. More importantly, he also learnt concerning facts such as that if The True One remained ill for too long, the world would be at risk of eroding and evaporating into thin air. Though it saddened him to admit it, he understood now why Reyan did what he did.

After reading dozens of more scrolls of this nature, Gabriel had achieved a complete understanding of the trouble his people were in. But in none of them was there even a hint of a solution as to how to save them. So far, Gabriel had only succeeded in speckling his hopeless depression with building frustration.

A sudden flash of light notified Gabriel from the corner of the room. His eyes darted over to the very end of the rows of stone-wall shelves where a ball of glowing energy was forming. If he did not know any better, he would think it was one of those spheres Aarush used to generate when he played with them as kids, it certainly bore a resemblance to them. All Gabriel knew was that it had to be a sign.

Gabriel followed the ball of light to the end of the stone shelves. When he arrived at the origin, the light itself dissipated and in its place, a scroll was there. Gabriel picked up and inspected the scroll. Constructed of a sturdier brown paper than any of the other scrolls, it was much longer with much more information.

"The Brew of Tranquillity?" Gabriel whispered as he read the title. He planted himself on the floor with force as he read the long winding scroll thoroughly. The more he read, the more his eyes widened and mood lightened. He had found exactly what he was looking for.

Magnolia sat on her bed, mindlessly staring at the leaves that decorated her wall as she twisted her platinum-white hair into knots. She had spent her whole day there from sunrise to sunset, barely moving, doing nothing but moping internally, her eyes blank. Magnolia looked at the scattered pile of discarded dirty clothes and items that made themselves into a depression pile in the corner of her room. Amongst the shirts, dresses, and sacks of old food packaging was an item that caught her interest again, a rusted crown with dried blood on it.

 She no longer wore that crown anymore. Nowadays it only acted as a reminder of worse times. Considering what the shelter was going through, she assumed even worse times were coming.

Magnolia heard a knock on her door. She was confused, as it was not common for her to get visitors at night. And she was not in the mood for any.

She opened the door to see a smiling Gabriel. Gabriel excitedly burst into Magnolia's room and sat on her bed. Magnolia noticed the beaming smile on his face and a thick scroll in his hands.

"What do you want, Gabriel?" Magnolia sighed.

"Remember when I said this all has to stop?"

"I do…"

"Well, I think I've figured out how it can." said Gabriel as he waved the scroll around. "With The Brew of Tranquillity."

For the first time that day, Magnolia was snapped out of her depressed lethargic state. She pulled her twig-twined chair from next to the window, placed it in front of Gabriel, and sat down.

"The Brew of Tranquillity?" Magnolia asked in intrigue.

Gabriel beamed with excitement as he un-scrolled the scroll. He shifted himself closer to Magnolia so she could also view the scroll as he went through it. He cleared his throat with passion.

"According to legend, deep within the Fourth Kingdom, there's this lake of immense tranquil properties sought after by both humans and novatus alike…"

As Gabriel explained the story of the Brew of Tranquillity, he manipulated wind in his one free hand and used it to act as a storyboard, just like how Aarush used to do so with fire when he was a kid. Magnolia watched in careful awe as Gabriel made an image of a lake's scenery with grey gusts of winds floating through her room.

"One day, many decades ago, a particularly powerful novatus had injured himself in battle and went to the lake to clean and potentially heal his wounds. But as his wounds healed…something else waned…". Gabriel's wind imagery showcased a large powerful man washing himself in the lake, only for the man to buckle down on his knees and for a glowing essence to leave his body.

"His novatus abilities started to drain from him, bringing him down to his knees. It is said that after stepping into the lake, this war-torn novatus felt twice as healthy, however, his powers were severely weakened. If he were of weaker ability, the lake would have consumed his life force almost entirely…"

"Interesting," commented Magnolia.

"That's not even the interesting part. Moments after, whilst he was still in the lake, the man was confronted by none other than The True One," said Gabriel as he shifted the wind imagery to showcase The True One landing by the lake and roaring at the man. The wind imagery of The True One started to chase the man around the lake, gulping in the water in an attempt to consume him. "Though the man was initially powerful enough to fight back, due to the lake depleting his novatus powers considerably he could do nothing but run away as The True One attempted to consume him. With its immense power and intense hunger, The True One unhinged its jaw and started to suction in the water of the lake, consuming it as it pulled the man in. But as The True One consumed more and more of the water, it started to calm. No longer did it want to consume the man or even kill him. In fact, after digesting the water affected by the novatus' abilities, it was said that The True One had never been more satisfied and spent the next couple of years calm and rested."

Gabriel's wind imagery showed The True One curled up into a ball, resting. He waved away the wind, concluding the story. Magnolia looked at the ground blankly, then back up at Gabriel."

"That's a very interesting story I suppose," said Magnolia. "I don't see how it helps us in any way shape or form-."

"That's where the Theory of the Brew of Tranquillity comes in." Gabriel interrupted as he tapped the writing on the scroll vigorously. "It's believed that the phenomenon that war-torn novatus accidentally caused could be intentionally replicated again one day. All that would be needed was one extremely powerful member of each of the six classes of novatus - Kin of Skies, Kin of Land, Kin of Sun, Kin of Moon, Kin of Man, and Kin of Beasts, to band together, travel to the lake and excrete their powers to make a brew that would satiate The True One for eternity…"

"Oh wow…that…that *could* very well solve everything!" Magnolia exclaimed, finally starting to match Gabriel's excitement. "But where could we find novatus powerful or willing enough to do that?"

Gabriel rolled up the scroll slowly, making strict eye contact with Magnolia the entire time. Magnolia stared into Gabriel's soft brown eyes confused. But as Gabriel's stare strengthened, Magnolia slowly came to the realisation.

"No!" she rejected emphatically. "You can't be serious!"

"Magnolia, think about it. I'm the most skilled Kin of Skies and you're the most skilled Kin of Land. With most of the Protectors either captured, killed, or injured it means that right now, we are the most powerful of our novatus class in the shelter and on the peninsula," explained Gabriel. "Meaning we have the potential to be the most powerful novatus not in hiding. It's either us, or no one."

"You want us to go on a perilous journey all the way to the Fourth Kingdom to risk our lives making some concoction for The True One?!"

"Um. Yeah."

"You're out of your mind!" exclaimed Magnolia. "Even if we wanted to do it, how would we find another four people to do it with us?"

"We also have Kane. He could join us to fill in the Kin of Sun role," suggested Gabriel. "And the other three, we can find along the way to our journey to the Fourth Kingdom."

"Kane? As in the same Kane no one has seen at the shelter in weeks?" asked Magnolia. Gabriel sighed, seeing Magnolia's point. The last any of them saw of Kane was that night at his and Gabriel's Novaldem two weeks ago. Since then, he had been a ghost at the peninsula.

"And then you want us to collect the other three along the way? I'm sorry Gabriel, but I don't think you've thought this through enough."

"Well, what else are we to do?! Just sit around letting our people get tortured by humans and killed by The True One!" exclaimed Gabriel.

"It's not that we shouldn't, it's that we can't," said Magnolia. "From what you told me in that story, none of us are powerful enough to help make the brew, not even Kane. We'd hurt ourselves. Or worse."

"So? We'll train every day! It's a long journey travelling from here to the Fourth Kingdom without being detected by humans. If we train twice a day along our journey, we'll be powerful enough to do it by the time we get there!" suggested Gabriel with passion. He stood there, waiting for Magnolia to answer.

"Not a chance," she sighed.

Gabriel groaned with frustration. He stood up from Magnolia's bed and walked over to slump himself by the wall. He sat there dejected, next to the depression pile of clothes in the corner of Magnolia's room.

As Magnolia turned to explain herself to him, her attention was directed back to the pile. The bloody crown caught her eye again. Her eyes shifted as they lay on the crown, the royal ornament evoking a reaction within her. She gulped down a large lump in her throat, sighing out of her nose.

"Fine," she said.

"Magnolia pl-. Wait what?" gasped Gabriel, immediately taken aback as if he had expected and was prepared for another argument.

"I said fine. Let's do it. Let's work our way towards making the Brew of Tranquillity…"

Gabriel's mouth dropped open and eyes widened to the point where they could have fallen out completely. Though this was the outcome he came into the room wanting to reach, he still could not believe what he was hearing. A wave of emotion immediately washed over Gabriel. His hands quivered, his lip trembled and his body shook as tears welled in his eyes.

"Are you okay?" asked Magnolia. Before he could answer, Gabriel lunged towards Magnolia and embraced her in the tightest of hugs.

"Thank you, Magnolia!" sighed Gabriel. "You don't know how much this means to me."

Magnolia smiled as she patted Gabriel on the back. The two broke their hug together and stared into each other's eyes for a moment. Something in Gabriel's eyes seemed to calm Magnolia, making her feel that perhaps, she might have made the right choice.

"What made you change your mind so quickly?" Gabriel asked.

"Nothing in particular." Magnolia lied. "It's like you said. This all has to stop."

SUNFIRE, MOONWATER

An elderly couple relaxing by the lake. Townsfolk congregating in salons. A child climbing a tree. No matter what he saw humans do as he soared through the First Kingdom, he hated it.

Engulfed in flames and flying through the dark early morning sky, any First Kingdom citizen would assume what was soaring above their heads was a blazing shooting star. Perhaps it was another odd phenomenon of The True One's effect on the world and nature, especially considering its state of sickness. But it was not. It was Kane Keahi, travelling through the skies. Kane was never one to waste the energy that granted him his novatus abilities, especially in such an inefficient manner. Yet for the past few days, he had been doing just that. There was somewhere he *desperately* needed to be.

***

That same morning, Gabriel and Magnolia were also travelling. But not via the skies, via the seas. It was the very beginning of their journey across the Kingdoms. With all their belongings packed in heavy sacks, Gabriel and Magnolia met up with each other by the docks of the peninsula, with plans to commandeer one of the few ships that had not already been destroyed. The two of them had decided to leave for the seas early in the morning without notifying anyone else in what was left of the peninsula's shelter. They were out to sea before anyone could realise what they planned to do, or convince them otherwise.

The ship Gabriel and Magnolia chose was not the most impressive of vessels. A standard wooden sailor's ship with two decks, an upper one where the ship was to be steered at the helm and allowed for the wind to flow through its sails and a lower deck with a series of rooms capable of food storage, cloth storage, and dozens of shipmates.

Using subtle air manipulation, Gabriel was able to make the ship move faster without touching the wheel, by allowing stronger gusts of wind to push the sails along. With a map of 'The Seas of the First Kingdom' in hand and a specific route marked on it in ink, Gabriel looked confident with how their journey was faring so far as he stood upon the upper deck. Magnolia looked quite the opposite.

"We've not made a mistake, have we?" Magnolia asked as she anxiously looked at the waves in the sea. "Coming out here and all?"

"No, we haven't…" Gabriel assured her, his eyes still fixated on the map.

"Right." Magnolia sighed, not sounding entirely convinced. "So where are we sailing first?"

"If we follow the route I have planned out, we should be able to stop off at the mainland of the First Kingdom in a few days without bumping into any humans trying to kill us. Hopefully."

"Why would we want to stop off at the mainland?" asked Magnolia.

"To look for Kane," Gabriel told her.

"You know where he is? For sure?" asked Magnolia.

"Well, I have a fair idea of where he *might* be," Gabriel said as he folded up the map emphatically.

"Better than nothing, I suppose," she sighed, leaning on the deck's railings.

Gabriel and Magnolia spent the next three days of their journey at sea switching between constant states of fear and boredom. The seas were rough and full of peril, but luckily, the two were able to keep the boat steady and themselves safe. In the meantime, they tried to make the most of their time on the ship, training their Kin of Skies and Kin of Land powers, eating, sleeping, and entertaining themselves as best they could.

The first day was the hardest. The ship was tossed about by the waves, and both Gabriel and Magnolia were prone to seasickness on alternating occasions. Gabriel used his Kin of Skies power to try to calm the winds and make the ship move more smoothly, though this only helped a little. As the day wore on, they both began to feel a bit better. They ate some dried fruit and biscuits that they had brought with them, calming their sickness. But as soon as they were both well, Gabriel insisted they compounded on further training, much to Magnolia's annoyance.

The second and third days were less troublesome and more boring. The ship moved steadily through the waves, as the two spent most of their time training their powers and trying to keep themselves occupied. Other than this, eating, and keeping each other entertained by sharing stories, not much happened that day at all. That all changed as the third night came.

That night, Gabriel kept his vigil on the deck, staring out into the churning waters as Magnolia lay in her cabin trying to find some respite from the endless swaying of the boat. She had finally managed to drift off to sleep, but it wasn't long before she was jolted awake by the sound of the ship being rocked violently by a wave.

Magnolia leapt out of bed in a panic, her heart racing as she stumbled towards the door. She could hear the sound of the sea crashing against the ship, and she knew that something was wrong. She burst onto the deck to find Gabriel struggling to use the wind and his Kin of Skies abilities to control and push back the waves.

"Gabriel?! What's going on?!" Magnolia shouted.

"Help me!" Gabriel shouted back at her.

Magnolia did not hesitate. Using her Kin of Land powers, she struggled to pull up strong vines from beneath the water's surface. She willed the vines to rise and combat the thrashing waves, hoping to aid Gabriel in fighting them off and protecting the boat.

But it was no use. The waves were far too strong for either of them to keep them at bay, water crashing at them from all directions. The ship was tossed and turned by the violent treacherous waters and before they knew it, the waves had crashed over the deck. A wall of water drenched itself over the two, carrying them with it as it sent them into the sea.

As they fell into the sea, Gabriel made efforts to use his power to manipulate the air and create a bubble of air around them, but it was no use. The pair were quickly pulled under the water. Soon their breath was stolen from them, then, their consciousness.

***

Magnolia woke up the next morning, rubbing her groggy eyes as she cursed herself under her breath - something that was quickly becoming her usual routine after regaining consciousness. "I need to stop doing this…"

As Magnolia fully opened her eyes and awakened, the first thing she saw was another young woman mindlessly playing with a couple of strands of her hair. The woman had large frizzy black hair that hung only a few centimetres over a couple of slim brown eyes that screamed mischief.

"Gosh, this hair is so fine and white." the frizzy-haired woman said as she marvelled at Magnolia's strands within her hands.

"What's going on, where am I right now?" asked Magnolia. "Who are you?"

"I've always wanted to do my hair in a similar style to this, you know," the woman said.

"Who are you?" Magnolia repeated.

"But I don't know if I could pull it off as well as you do, not with my hair texture." the woman continued.

"What?" Magnolia gasped in confusion. She reviewed her surroundings to see that although the cave they were in was dry and filled with air, when she looked outside of the cave entrance, she saw nothing but a wall of imposing seawater.

"Where am I? What's happening here?!" Magnolia panicked. The woman chose not to answer her question, but to instead, laugh at her. Magnolia's face twisted with confusion.

As she looked around her surroundings, she spotted Gabriel groggily getting up from the other side of the cave.

"Oh nice, the other one's awake now," said the woman. As soon as Gabriel locked eyes with her, he defaulted to attack mode.

"Who are you and what is this place?" Gabriel asked, generating a sword out of air, and threatening the woman with it.

"Is everyone just going to keep asking the same questions?" she groaned. Gabriel grunted at her. He manipulated the air to make the sword twice as big and pointed it at her neck. The woman sighed.

"Fine. My name is Selene. Selene Lila Abano if you want to get all specific. Are you happy?"

"That only answers one of my questions. So, no. I'm not happy." Gabriel said, pushing the air blade closer to Selene's neck.

"Calm down, we're all friends here." Selene chuckled.

"No, we're not! We've just met you!" Magnolia exclaimed.

"Aw yeah, true." Selene accepted. "Let me introduce myself, my name is Selene Lila-"

"We know that already!" Gabriel and Magnolia exclaimed at her in unison.

"Oh yeah that's right…" Selene laughed. "What was the other question again?"

Gabriel groaned with deep frustration. Magnolia facepalmed so hard it smacked a red mark on her forehead.

"You know guys, you're both awfully rude for people whose lives I saved by dragging in here. I didn't have to do this, you know!" complained Selene, blowing a raspberry at the two. Gabriel and Magnolia shared a somewhat ashamed look.

"You're right, we're sorry," said Magnolia.

"That's better." scoffed Selene.

"Can you tell us where we are now?" Gabriel asked. "Last thing I remember was seawater filling my lungs. But now, we're breathing air?"

"All I did was clear out the water from these caves and stop it just before it comes inside."

"But how?"

"Because I'm a Kin of Moon, duh," Selene chuckled. "I'm a novatus, just like you guys."

Selene pointed to the jagged birthmark on their collars, poking through both their tattered clothes. She then pulled down the collar of her shirt slightly to show off hers.

Gabriel and Magnolia shared another look amongst each other, but this time, a more positive vibe about them. Gabriel extinguished his air sword and instead used his hand to offer Selene a handshake.

"Sorry if we got off on the wrong foot. I'm Gabriel and that's Magnolia." Gabriel told her. "You don't understand how pleased we are that you weren't some humans trying to hunt us.

"Okay," Selene laughed as she accepted Gabriel's handshake.

"You said you were a Kin of Moon, didn't you Selene?" Magnolia asked.

"That I am," she confirmed.

Magnolia raised an eyebrow at Gabriel. He shook his head at her. "I don't think so."

"Why not?"

"Because we barely know her! We only found out her name a minute ago!"

"Come on, Gabriel, what are the chances that days after we embark on our journey, we not only stumble upon but have our lives saved by a Kin of Moon?" asked Magnolia. "If there ever was a sign from the universe, this is it! We should at least think about asking her to come along!"

"Ooh, yes, definitely! I want to come along on the adventure!" exclaimed Selene.

"You don't even know what the adventure is!" Gabriel exclaimed back.

"I still want to go!" said Selene. "Everything is so boring down here all on my own."

"You stay down here on your own?" Gabriel asked.

"Yep! Come to think of it, you guys are the first people I've had down here in ages that weren't some human hunters trying to kill me!" Selene laughed. She grasped her belly as she incessantly chortled at her own remarks. Gabriel and Magnolia shared yet another concerned look. Gabriel grabbed Magnolia by the arm, taking her aside to talk in private.

"I'll be honest, Magnolia. I'm not sure about this, I'm not sure about this at all."

"Neither am I, but I still think she'd make a good addition."

"Really?"

The two looked back at Selene to see that she was using her Kin of Moon powers to create humanoid shadows whom she made chase her around the cave like a dog chasing its tail.

"Well, not really," Magnolia admitted. "But if you think about it, she's perfect for the situation we're currently in.

"How?!" asked Gabriel.

"Look around Gabriel! She's a Kin of Moon with powerful enough abilities to block the seawater from coming into this cave!" Magnolia explained. "If there's anyone who can help us make our way back to the ship and contribute to the Brew of Tranquillity it's her!"

Gabriel glanced back at Selene who was still laughing her heart away with the many shadows following her. Despite what he saw, his face squirmed as if he was being swayed.

"I'll be honest with *you*, Gabriel, I'm still not convinced that we didn't make a mistake by embarking on this ridiculous journey. Especially with our journey across the seas so far." Magnolia admitted. Gabriel tensed his jaw, taken aback and offended by the remark but willing to listen.

"But if there's one thing, we can do to set things back on course? It's letting this Selene girl 'come along'."

Gabriel took a second to digest what Magnolia said. With his hands on his hips, he looked to the ground.

"Selene…" he called out.

"Yes?" Selene answered, taking a moment to stop her game of shadow catch.

"I changed my mind…" Gabriel said. "…you can join us on our 'adventure'."

Selene's face beamed with delight.

"Yes!" Selene celebrated, jumping, and pumping her fist in the air. "Alright, when do we leave for it? Now? Tomorrow? Ten minutes? Now?"

"Don't you want to find out what the adventure is first?" asked Magnolia.

"Oh, right yeah of course," said Selene. She frantically sat herself down and crossed her legs like a kid ready to listen to a story. "Go on, tell me."

"Very well..." Gabriel sighed as he glanced at Magnolia. "Where do we start?"

***

Together, Magnolia and Gabriel spent the following four minutes explaining to Selene what they were trying to achieve in terms of the Brew of Tranquillity...then the four minutes following that explaining it to her again as she had not been listening the first time around. Eventually, the two managed to catch her up to speed, and once they were done, she looked even more inconceivably excited than she was before.

"Yes! Let's do it!" screamed Selene.

"Are you sure you're up for it all?" Magnolia asked her. "This is a very dangerous mission and-"

"Yes! Let's go make that damn Brew! YEAH! WOOO!" Selene celebrated at the top of her lungs. Magnolia chuckled at Selene's excitement. Even Gabriel could not help but smile.

"Well, first. We need to get back to our boat," said Gabriel.

"Oh yeah, obviously." realised Selene. She ran across the cave and towards the wall of water that led them back to the ocean. Using her Kin of Moon abilities, Selene parted a section of the water and created a tunnelled passageway for them to walk through. "Come on, let's go find it! Quick!"

She sprinted down the passageway she created. Magnolia and Gabriel followed her down it, though the latter with a reluctance about it. Magnolia smiled warmly.

"I think we'll grow to like our new teammate," she said.

"Let's hope so…" Gabriel groaned.

Selene led Gabriel and Magnolia through the narrow passageway, the sound of rushing water echoing around them. As they emerged into the open, she gasped in awe at the beauty that lay before them. The sea stretched out endlessly, its waters crystal clear and teeming with life. Schools of fish darted past, their scales glittering in the sunlight that filtered down from above.

"Look at this," Selene said, her voice full of wonder. "One of the only good things about living down here…sometimes the sea is its own wonderful world."

Gabriel and Magnolia nodded in agreement with her as they watched in wonder.

As they passed through the water, they saw the bottom of other ships from below. As Selene herself looked up at them, she gulped, visibly scared and shaking.

"Are you good?" asked Gabriel.

"Of course," Selene laughed awkwardly.

Finally, they reached the spot where according to Selene, she had seen them 'lamely plummet into the sea.' She searched with her eyes, and after a short while, Magnolia excitedly spotted it from above. "There it is!" she exclaimed.

With help from Gabriel, Selene turned the passageway into an air bubble, and they ascended above the water's surface to get a better view of their ship. But as soon as they spotted it, their joy turned to shock as they saw their previously empty vessel occupied by a group of outlaws. With leather waistcoats and baggy white trousers on board, they drank their fill and sang their songs. They were rough, rowdy, and held together twenty strong. If they did not know any better, they would assume that this boat had belonged to those outlaws all along from how quickly they had made it their home.

"What the hell? Who are these people?" asked Gabriel. "And why are they on our boat?"

"Remember when I said human hunters came around here sometimes?" Selene asked.

"Yeah," they both replied.

"Well, there they are," Selene said, her voice barely above a whisper. "If I were you guys, I'd be scared shitless right now…"

SUNFIRE, MOONWATER II

"Are those novatus hunters?" Gabriel asked.

Selene shook her head. "Nope, they're just undersea Gold-Hunters...who also happen to hunt novatus sometimes."

"Fantastic," Gabriel sighed sarcastically.

"There's so many of them," said Magnolia. "I don't think we'll be able to fight them off."

"You're right, we'll have to take a different approach." planned Gabriel. "I say we wait here for a short while until they finish drinking, then when the moment is opportun-"

Before Gabriel could even come up with a full plan, Selene surprised them both by using her Kin of Moon powers to propel them out of their water bubble and shoot them right onto the boat. The trio landed right smack in the middle of all the Gold-Hunters' celebrations on the front deck. Caught off guard, the Gold-Hunters immediately started to cuss out the three, instantly resorting to shouting at them.

Ignoring their incomprehensible threats, Selene pointed at the men who stood in front of her.

"Hey, you guys. Get off my friends' ship please," she told them casually.

An awkward silence encapsulated the entire upper deck for a moment. A chorus of mocking laughter came soon after. Once again, the Gold-Hunters snarled and threw more profanities the trio's way, their voices increasing in volume and violence. The trio huddled closer together in the middle of the deck as the hunters closed in on them.

"Why would you make us jump into this so quickly?!" Gabriel complained.

"Yeah, what happened to you being shit scared to see them?!" Magnolia added.

"Aren't people supposed to like, face their fears?" Selene asked.

"Now is not the time for that!" Gabriel chastised. In response, Selene could only muster up a shrug, much to his chagrin.

As they turned to face the Gold-Hunters, they saw the group of rough-faced men with greasy hair and ragged clothes continue to close in on them. Their leader, a grizzled man with the bushiest beard and largest cutlass on deck, stepped forward.

"This is our boat now," he snarled. "Why don't you get off before we kill ya, okay?"

"No thank you," Selene responded nonchalantly.

The leader laughed. He raised his cutlass in threat to Selene, more than ready to slice her down. Though her body was shivering and her eyes were quivering, Selene stood her ground in front of the man, weapons, and all. Before the leader could make good on his threat, one of his subordinates held his arm back.

"Are you mad?!" the leader snarled at the subordinate.

"No boss, it's just that…this girl and her friends just propelled themselves out of the damn water."

"So?"

"So, these aren't just some regular kids who took a ship out to sea. These are novatus." his subordinate explained to him. "Why kill them when we can capture and sell them to the Vyre for a pretty profit?"

The leader's bloodshot eyes shone bright with realisation. A wicked smile slithered onto his face.

"You're absolutely right! Bring them boys!" he ordered. On that note, more of the gold hunters unsheathed their cutlasses, laughing and snarling all the more.

"No chance," Gabriel grunted back at the leader. Huddled together, back-to-back, the trio took up fighting stances. Gabriel generated wind around him, Selene raised water from the ocean and Magnolia prepared her vines from the seabed as the Gold-Hunters charged their way towards them with bloody swishing cutlasses.

***

The battle of the top deck was a chaotic one from the very beginning. Gabriel and Magnolia had experience fighting against multiple human swordsmen before, but the untrained fighting style of the Gold-Hunters made it difficult for them to predict the movements of their wild cutlass slashes.

Learning from her mistakes back at Reyan's raid, Magnolia formed protective vines to block her from being stabbed, with more precision than her earth walls. She and Gabriel worked in tandem to utilise their abilities together, standing back-to-back at the front of the deck as they let groups of Gold-Hunters surround them.

With the gold hunters all around them in a circle, the two spun around with their backs together sending plant and air-based attacks to each of the hunters who descended upon them in a continuous circle of elemental martial arts.

Selene, in spite of her body still shaking with fear, fought with surprising skill and bravery, using her water manipulation to create waves and launch high-pressure streams at the Gold-Hunters. Her shadow energy manipulation allowed her to slip in and out of the shadows, making it difficult for the gold-hunters to keep track of her, whilst using the natural advantage of having the ocean around her, to dowse and incapacitate many more Gold-Hunting opponents than the other two combined.

Though her abilities allowed her to fight effectively, they did not allow for her to fight cleanly, with many of her attacks dispersing further than she would have liked them to have. The erratic nature of her abilities was soon becoming a problem. The waves she sent across the boat, though they targeted Gold-Hunters, started to wash over Magnolia and even knock down Gabriel. Selene's waterworks did well to take down the Gold-Hunters the two were fighting but also came close to knocking Gabriel off of the boat entirely.

"Selene, calm down!" Gabriel shouted, trying to get through to her. "You're going to throw us off of the ship!"

Despite Gabriel's warnings, Selene continued to fight off the remaining Gold-Hunters in the same erratic manner, now intertwining dark shadows with water. At this point, the other two were forced to cramp by the railings at the front of the deck just to avoid getting struck by her.

"Selene!" Magnolia called out to her desperately, at the top of her lungs.

Selene was too focused on taking down the Gold-Hunters to listen to her teammates. Gabriel and Magnolia found themselves barely able to keep a stable footing as Selene's darkness-induced waves threatened to capsize the entire vessel. Dozens of Gold-Hunters saw themselves knocked off of the ship completely, dropping like flies into the sea below to drown. Magnolia entangled her body and the railing in sturdy sea vines to prevent herself from falling off the side. Gabriel however had no such luck and like the Gold-Hunters, he found himself knocked off the ship and thrusted down into the sea.

***

Gabriel sank deeper into the water, his lungs burning with the need for air. He looked around frantically, seeing the shapes of the Gold-Hunters sinking alongside him. And then, he spotted the leader sinking nearby. The man's eyes widened in recognition and he lunged at Gabriel with murderous intent. Gabriel struggled to push the man away, but the water made it difficult to move quickly. The Gold-Hunter's hands closed tightly around Gabriel's throat, squeezing the air out of his lungs. Panic set in as Gabriel realised, he was going to die, and there was nothing he could do to stop it.

The Gold-Hunter suddenly convulsed and released his grip on Gabriel. A water spear jutted out from the man's head, and he went still. Gabriel stared in shock, realising that Selene had used her water powers to save him. He felt a surge of energy propel him upward, breaking the surface of the water. Selene had brought him back onto the boat again. Coughing and gasping for air, he looked around to see Magnolia and Selene on the ship, both also coughing and spluttering.

Selene used her dark energy to carry the dead Gold-Hunters off the ship and dump them into the water. Once done, Selene dusted her hands together as if to signify a job well done, oblivious to the fact that the other two were not in a completely healthy state.

"Nice. Now we have a boat." Selene celebrated. "Well, now I have a boat. Technically you guys already had one."

"Were you trying to kill us?!" Gabriel chastised.

"No, I was trying to kill them, silly." Selene laughed as she pointed to the drowning Gold-Hunters in the water.

"But you almost made us collateral," Magnolia complained. "Didn't you hear us telling you to calm down?"

"Yeah, but I was in the zone," Selene explained. "Sorry. I'll try to make sure not to almost kill you as much in the next fight."

Gabriel's face twisted into the most angered of scowls directed at Selene, who was too nonchalant to notice. Magnolia sighed, facepalming at her for the second time that day.

Gabriel and Magnolia spent the rest of their day continuing their journey en route to the mainland of the First Kingdom, this time with Selene by their side. Though Selene's abilities proved a great aid in pushing the ship along faster, she mostly disrupted their daily routine. Selene messily ate the fruit and biscuits they packed like a rabid animal and once she was done with her food, poked, and prodded at theirs.

When it came time for training, Selene often either lost focus or refused to participate altogether. Not to mention the times when she would intentionally use her powers to make the seawater below them wilder and more dangerous to 'make the journey less boring.'

After all of this, it was no surprise that Gabriel sought an early night, tired from it all and wanting to get away from her.

***

That night, Gabriel dreamt sweet dreams of fond memories of events long gone by. He found himself as a young boy again, back in the first novatus shelter he had ever been in. Back in the wooded shelter. A young Gabriel frolicked through fields of tall grass, giggling with sweet childlike innocence. On either side of Gabriel were Dillon and Maximilian who ran and giggled along with him. With a warm smile, Protector Aarush watched from the end of the field, waiting for them to run to him.

Being the youngest of them all Gabriel ran the slowest. To catch up with his friends, Gabriel sprinted as hard as he could, only to end up hurting his feet and falling over to the floor. Young Gabriel cried as he held his hurt foot. It took a few moments for them to realise, but once they did, Dillon and Max tracked back to get him again. As soon as they arrived, Max laughed at Gabriel, realising he had come out running with no shoes. Gabriel frowned downwards in shame. Using his Kin of Man abilities, Dillon immediately got to work collecting grass and weaving them into workable shoes for Gabriel to wear within seconds. He took the shoes and carefully placed them on his bare feet, astonishing young Gabriel with such a skilful act of kindness. With a pat on the back, Max pulled Gabriel back up to his feet. The three boys were back to laughing and giggling as they ran across the field and into Protector Aarush's arms.

The dream abruptly ended, Gabriel awakening from his sleep with tears in his eyes.

Unable to sleep, Gabriel made his way back up to the upper deck to see who was taking watch. Gabriel climbed up the wooden stairs from the lower deck cabin and up through the compartment to the top deck. The first thing he saw past the helm was that it was Selene and not Magnolia keeping watch. He crouched down to try and silently slink away before Selene could see him. But as Selene turned around, he saw he was too late.

"Oh, hey Gabriel." Selene greeted him in a sombre tone. Gabriel observed her body language and facial expression. Gone was the usually irreverent and off-the-wall energy Selene had been exhibiting from the moment they met her. Almost as if the energy had been syphoned out of her. This compelled him to walk onto the deck proper and join her side.

"Is something wrong?" Gabriel asked her.

"No, I'm just thinking," Selene told him as she looked out to sea. "This is what I look like when I think."

"Oh, okay," Gabriel said. He joined her in silently staring at the sea, not a word exchanged between the two for moments on end.

But then, Selene turned away from the sea and towards him. Her smile returned to her face.

"You know, I'm really glad you two randomly showed up," Selene told him. "I never would have had the courage to defeat the Gold-Hunters if I was on my own."

"Really?" asked Gabriel, a pleased smirk growing on his face.

"Yeah." laughed Selene. "You guys being here finally gave me an excuse to at least try."

"I'm glad we could help with that," Gabriel said, smiling back at her. "But if I'm being honest, something confuses me about all this."

"What?"

"Why were you living on your own down there in the first place?"

"That's a good question." laughed Selene. "But to answer, I'd kind of have to tell you the stupid story that comes with it."

"So?" asked Gabriel. "I'm more than willing to listen."

Selene raised an eyebrow as she looked at Gabriel. She was met with wondrous genuine eyes that she could not help but smile in the presence of. She let out a deep breath and started her story.

"I've spent almost all my life underwater. I grew up with a clan of novatus, all Kin of Moon, all nomads who lived a free lifestyle in these underwater villages, kind of like the cave I brought you guys to but much larger and interconnected. I was born into a group of people who had lived this way for decades. The sea is all they knew."

"Never knew there were people like that," Gabriel marvelled. "What was it like living with them?"

"Honestly, I can barely remember," Selene chuckled as she continued the story. "I was a sickly child so I barely got to look around at anything, never mind travel through the villages. I spent most of my time resting in the healing pool in one of the caves. The elders would bring food and water and tell me stories as I rested there. I can barely remember a moment in time in which I wasn't cooped up within that cave…wallowing away in that pool…"

"Oh, I'm sorry to hear that," said Gabriel.

"That's not the part you should be sorry to hear," Selene laughed.

Gabriel's eyebrows furrowed as he watched Selene giggle to herself.

"I remember being stuck in the healing pool one day when the entrance to my cave crumbled beneath me. I was confused and scared, really scared. Stone and rock had randomly fallen and sealed me there and I was too weak and sick to do anything about it…"

Selene paused for a moment, almost choking on her words. Gabriel looked over at her with sympathetic eyes.

"…it was only a couple of years ago when I could finally muster up the strength to not need the healing pool. By then the wall of debris had started to erode and I could break free. I was able to escape and found out that my entire village had been chased away, following a struggle involving the undersea Gold-Hunters. I pieced together that the stone that accidentally sealed me within the cave was actually debris from the villages that were ransacked, destroyed, broken down, and washed away through the sea. But before I escaped? Before I found out? All I knew was that I was trapped, and for years I could do nothing about it. And even after I was able to escape, I decided to stay in my cave. For what reason? I'm not sure. I guess it's because the sea was all I knew…"

Selene hung her head in sadness, letting out the deepest of sighs as she finished the story. Without hesitation, Gabriel placed his hands around her shoulder to comfort her.

"I can't imagine how terrible that must have been to live through," he sighed. "Now I feel bad for being so snippy with you after you saved us and all. I owe you another apol-"

Selene interrupted Gabriel's profuse apologies with intense hearty laughter, startling him aback. Her excitable nature had returned in an instant.

"You don't owe me anything, Gabriel! If anything, I *owe* you! Like I said, because of you guys I have a reason to at least try to brave the world again!" she exclaimed with vigour. "Seeing other novatus like you guys travelling to places they don't know means I have no excuse not to do the same!"

Selene pumped both her fists in the air triumphantly. "Sure, that whole Brew of Tranquillity Journey sounds like a batshit insane idea, but I'm willing to do it! Not just for me but for all of us! Once we're done, novatus will be able to travel wherever they want, whenever they want, to their heart's fucking content!"

A tear almost came to Gabriel's eyes as he watched her pump her fists in the air. "Selene...I don't think there are any words I could use to describe how happy I am to hear you say that."

"Really? How about, I'm super-duper extra uber glad to have someone as wonderful as you joining me, Selene?" she suggested irreverently.

Gabriel laughed. "Yes. I'm super-duper extra uber glad to have someone as wonderful as you joining me, Selene," he said.

Selene grinned from ear to ear. She rested her head on Gabriel's shoulder as the two of them looked deep out into the seas of the night.

***

Whilst Selene and Gabriel were having their moment of novatus triumph, humans were having a triumph of their own within the heart of the First Kingdoms. Those of the highest standing gathered at a long table in the dining room of the finest palaces in the entire nation.

The dining room was an opulent sight to behold. There was a long table as exquisitely polished as the guests who sat at it, young and old. They wore the finest attire, with satin robes and pearly jewels that sparkled brighter than the chandeliers that hung above as they ate.

An indulgent young man sat at the head of the table, a kingly crown on his head and a lecherous look on his face - The infamous Franz

Kaymore, Grand Leader of the First Kingdom. The royal sat directly across another leader at the end of the table - Nathanael Reyan of the Vyre.

***

Half an hour into the banquet, The Grand Leader drunkenly stood up from his seat and raised a chalice of wine triumphantly.

"To Nathanael Reyan!" he toasted. "Not just for his efforts in dealing with the novatus and pleasing The True One …but for allowing us to host such an epic feast in his honour!"

"Thank you, Grand Leader Franz," said Reyan with quiet dignity.

"Cheers to Nathanael!" The Grand Leader shouted.

"Cheers to Nathanael!" shouted the guests at the table as they raised their chalices. The table gave a massive round of applause in celebration of Reyan. He stared ahead stoically, completely unmoved by the praise bestowed upon him, and simply waited for it to die down.

"And now, time for the entertainment!" declared Grand Leader Franz much to the excitement of the entire room. Soon the door burst open and knight-guards of the palace poured in. Dragged into the room behind the knights, with heavy locks and chains that bound their hands together were a group of novatus slaves. Shirtless men with scars on their backs and sadness on their faces as they were corralled around the table. The room was filled with grand laughter as the knights paraded them in front of the guests. All of the aristocracy chuckled and chortled at the novatus slaves' expense.

All but Reyan, who silently watched in disgust.

CLAN OF CAELESTIS

As the first beams of sunlight rose over the horizon, the trio's ship finally reached the shores of a First Kingdom Island. From the top deck, Gabriel soared into the sky, scanning the area for any signs of humans. He sighed with relief upon seeing not one within the general vicinity, more than happy to relay the information to Magnolia and Selene.

Below, the three were greeted by the many sounds and smells of the forest that lay ahead of them past the short beach shore. The forest was dense and cluttered, with trees of all shapes and sizes and foliage so thick that sunlight barely made it through the canopy.

Magnolia manipulated the vines and leaves around them, growing them to such an extent that they blanketed the ship, leaving it almost completely hidden. With that done, the trio climbed across a vine Magnolia stretched out onto the forest floors. As the trio landed, they took their first steps on dry land in days. Or for Selene, years.

"We're here!" Selene exclaimed excitedly.

"We're here," Magnolia repeated with a smile.

"We're here…" Gabriel sighed, gulping down a lump in his throat.

***

Early that morning, the festivities of the banquet from the night prior were still running their hedonistic course, courtesy of Grand Leader Franz Kaymore's utter refusal to cease the celebrations. Half of the aristocrats who had joined them at the start of the banquet had taken leave already, including Nathanael Reyan, the man whom the banquet was initially for. Only the drunkest and most indulgent of the kingdom's aristocracy remained dancing and frolicking around the room, making their best efforts to thrash the space. As well as the aristocracy, the novatus slaves were still in the dining room entertaining the guests, though not by choice. The rich party guests mocked and toyed with the chained-up men, slapping them, prodding them, throwing food in their faces and drinks at their feet.

"Dance you blasphemous creatures! Dance!" cheered Franz Kaymore as he sat in his chair throwing wine at the chained slaves across the room. "Where's my favourite one? Where's Enzo?!"

Two of the knight-guards unlinked one of the slaves from their chains but kept the binds on their hands. The slave was tall, tanned, and slim but muscled. Under other circumstances, 'Enzo' would have appeared to be a handsome and imposing figure, but as he was placed in front of The Grand Leader, all anyone could see was a battered and beaten novatus slave.

"Behold!" Kaymore shouted at the top of his lungs, grasping the attention of the other indulgent aristocrats. "They call these - Kin of Skies!"

"Ooh, Kin of Skies, those are my favourite!" said one of the female aristocrats. Soon a group of humans gathered around Kaymore and Enzo.

"Go on! Show us a trick!" ordered Kaymore. His booming voice caused Enzo to jump a little, amusing all the onlookers.

"But-, but I can't sir," Enzo said timidly.

"Eh? And why's that!"

"Because my hands are bound. I can't use my abilities with my hands bound."

"Well figure it out, dumbass! We're waiting here!" bellowed Kaymore. He swung a mailed fist, smacking the back of Enzo's head. In a panic, Enzo forced himself to use his abilities without his hands. After a while of tirelessly attempting to blow air out of his mouth, Enzo was finally able to muster something - a thin flow of grey wind. Kaymore smiled, waving his hands, and showcasing him to the crowd.

"Oh wow!" marvelled one of the male aristocrat onlookers.

"I know right?" agreed another.

As Enzo continued to blow the weak grey wind, Kaymore grabbed him by the back of his neck and forced him downwards. The Grand Leader removed his left foot from out of its jewel-encrusted shoe and brought it upwards. With an iron grip on his neck, Kaymore forced Enzo to blow in on his bare foot.

"Ahhhh, isn't that refreshing!" Kaymore laughed as he wiggled his toes. The room was quickly filled with the mocking laughs of aristocrats who threw wine and food down at Enzo again. The unfortunate Kin of Skies could do nothing but whimper at the feet of his oppressor.

***

Elsewhere, upon the dry scorched desert floors of the outer First Kingdom, novatus enjoyed a freedom greater than those in the Grand

Leaders Palace. Though these groups of novatus appeared almost as hardened and miserable. Donned in all-black tunics, twenty of them stood together in the middle of the desert. The group of hardened face ne'er-do-wells waited patiently in place as another novatus dressed in a black tunic and holding a large sack approached them. The sack-carrying novatus marched his way up to the forerunner of the group, a stout muscular man with tribal tattoos on his face, stopping just in front of him. The tattooed forerunner gave him an upwards nod. Upon this prompt, the man dumped out the contents of the sack. Raining down from it came the severed head of a Vyre shoulder with the tongue scorched red, eyes plunged out and a sun and star carved into the forehead in blood. The tattooed man smirked at the gruesome sight.

"It seems you're quick to prove your worth, Mr Keahi..." the tattooed man growled in a low voice. "... thus, it is my pleasure to welcome you to the Clan of Caelestis."

Kane bowed down to the clan members with gratitude. He rose back up to face them with a devilish glint in his eyes.

**

"Wait, so where are we going exactly?" Selene asked as the trio emerged from the other side of the forest and onto a field of yellow grass.

"Kicen Village," Gabriel muttered; his nose buried in his map again.

"Kicen Village?" asked Selene. "What the hell is Kicen Village?"

"A place I read about in one of the scrolls," Gabriel said, quickly dismissing her. Selene waited for further elaboration from Gabriel, only for him to continue to bury his nose in the map.

"Apparently, it's a hidden village for novatus," Magnolia explained. "Though I've only heard about it in legend, so ask Gabriel, he's the one who insisted we look there first."

"It's real," Gabriel insisted. "We should find it somewhere around here."

"So, is that where your friend Kang is?" asked Selene.

"Kane." Gabriel corrected. "And I think so."

"You're not sure?"

"Not as much as I'd like to be."

"Then why the hell are we looking for it?"

"Do you have a better idea of where we could be looking right now, Selene?"

"Yes."

"Really?"

"No."

"Then please be quiet." Gabriel groaned as he looked at the map. Selene turned to Magnolia with an exaggerated frown on her face. Magnolia shrugged back at her.

The trio walked along the stretch of seemingly never-ending yellow grass for longer than any of them would have wanted. The grass field built itself up to a hill then down to slope then up to a hill then down to a slope over and over. Every five minutes Gabriel would look up from the map and around at his surroundings in hopes of a landmark and every five minutes, he would find nothing. With an hour having passed and still a third of the field left to walk through, Gabriel's frustration was reaching greater heights than the hill they were on.

"The map says it should be around here! Why can't we find it anywhere?" complained Gabriel.

"Wouldn't be much of a hidden village if it wasn't hidden, would it?" snarked Magnolia

"You know what I mean." groaned Gabriel. "There should at least be something around here that could hint us to where it is."

"I wouldn't get your hopes up." Magnolia sighed.

"I have an idea of how we could find it," said Selene.

"Do you actually?" asked Gabriel Selene nodded in confirmation.

"KICEN! KICEN VILLAGE!" she screamed at the top of her lungs.

Magnolia's eyebrows furrowed. "Selene, what on Earth are you-"

"KICEN! KICEN VILLAGE!" Selene continued to call out.

Gabriel glared at Selene, breathing out of his nose heavily. "I don't get it, how does-"

"KICEN! KICEN VILLAGE!" Selene continued to scream, with her hands cupped around her mouth to make an echo.

"How does doing that help us find the village?" Gabriel asked, only to be ignored by Selene once again.

"KICEN! KICEN VILLAGE!"

With an abrupt crackling force, the earth beneath the trio immediately gave way. Before a single one of them could even as much as gasp, mud walls closed in over them as they were plunged into subterranean depths of darkness. The trio screamed as they were hurtled downwards beneath the earth, their pitch-black surroundings refusing to give them the slightest hint as to wherever they were being taken. An unknown force dragged them further and further down the ground, deeper into darkness until…it stopped.

The mud walls that encapsulated the trio retreated back to the grounds they came from. With the darkness cleared, their eyes adjusted, allowing them to see where they had been transported.

In front of them, Gabriel, Magnolia, and Selene saw the front of a humble rural settlement. The area had all the hallmarks of a small village. A centre with a well, a circular neighbourhood of homes rowed in the distance and small markets to the side. Unlike a normal village, most of these fixtures were constructed completely from earth and mud.

Stood in the village centre, in between the well and the trio themselves were a dozen villagers all dressed in different variations of a green-coloured tunic. Gabriel's eyes immediately fixated on the villager that stood in the middle of this group.

An exceptionally tall, gruff, and stone-featured man with arms folded and a glare lasering in at them.

"He looks friendly," Selene whispered to the other two. Magnolia rolled her eyes.

"You people are novatus, correct?" asked the man.

Gabriel lifted down his shirt collar to showcase his birthmark. "Correct."

"Good," the man grunted in response to him. "Then I don't have to kill you."

"And who are you exactly?" Magnolia asked, her voice equal parts meek and demanding.

"Teo Sten," the man answered proudly. "Leader of Kicen Village."

He continued to size up the trio, and more members of the village left their homes to see their arrival. Soon the three of them were looking upon a great number of novatus villagers huddled together.

From every window in every room on the top floor of the First Kingdoms Grand Castle, one could gaze upon the wide-open seas of the kingdom's entrance shore in all its glory. Anyone viewing such a scene from such a vantage point would consider themselves privileged for being able to adore such sights. Anyone but Enzo.

Though he held a room on the prestigious top floor of the castle, it looked nothing like the rest. It was less of a room with a window and more of a cruel stone enclosure with a hole in the wall to remind one of their lack of freedom. Enzo had spent many a day, chained to the wall of this 'room,' with nothing to do other than stare out of this window blankly.

"Reminiscing, are you?" Grand Leader Kaymore asked.

Enzo turned around to see his owner, mocking him as he leaned against the opened stone door. "Thinking back to times when you were a free little novie and not my fave prisoner of war, aren't you?"

"No sir." Enzo denied meekly.

"Don't lie, I know that look when I see it," said Kaymore. "Though I suppose it's harmless. Those days are long past you."

"Right sir," Enzo agreed, hanging his head in sadness.

***

Only a day had passed since his initial induction yet Kane was thrown into the deep end, forced to embark on his first mission as a member of the 'Clan of Caelestis.' Though the mission could barely have been described as a gruelling one, not by Kane's standards at least.

That afternoon, ten members of the Caelestis Clan including Kane had been tasked with infiltrating an abandoned church of humans and wiping them out. As far as Kane was concerned, it was not work, it was *play*. He could not even remember how many humans he had burnt the skin off of with his fire or blinded with his light.

As the clan members gathered together in the desert, sitting on stones around a campfire as they ate a post-mission meal of meat and beer, Kane still smirked to himself as he continuously recalled the 'fond memories' of their attacks on humans. The other clan members found themselves greatly amused by his attitude to their work.

"You're fitting in well." laughed a fine dark skinned female clan member who sat by him.

"What can I say? I enjoy being part of the cause." Kane chuckled.

"Too fucking right," she chuckled back. Raising her wooden mug of beer, she clashed it against Kane's in an act of comradery.

"So, when do I get to meet him?" Kane asked the woman.

"Meet who?"

"The leader. Mr Caelestis."

"What's with the rush new-boy? You'll meet 'Mr. Caelestis' when you're ready to meet him," she said. "Which, if you're lucky, might be real soon. But I wouldn't cream my pants about it just yet."

Kane shook his head and scoffed. He took a swig of beer, then glanced up towards the beating. That glistening look of hatred in his eyes shun even brighter than before.

WELCOME TO KICEN VILLAGE

A few hours into their stay there and Selene was already willing to stay there forever. After years of eating fish underwater and days of eating fruit and biscuits on the ship, even the dry somewhat shabby meals of soup and meat that Teo and the Kiceners had treated them to tasted golden to her.

The trio were surprised at how much hospitality they received as Teo took them further into the village. After a brief tour of the farm fields and a few odd discussions with the meek but kind village members, Teo took the trio into his own home.

They sat on a stone-mud-based, yet surprisingly soft sofa that protruded out of the floor in the earthy space that was his parlour room. Gabriel sat in between Magnolia and Selene with a small sack of scrolls and maps by his feet. Teo himself sat on a makeshift throne of polished dirt across from them as he sipped tea from a stone mug.

"It's always nice to see more novatus," Teo told them.

"It's nice for you to welcome us," Gabriel beamed.

"Where do you hail from?" Teo asked.

"The sea," Selene answered deadpan. Teo scowled at her in confusion.

"Gabriel and I are from The Novatus Peninsula Protection Centre. We met Selene along our journey here," explained Magnolia.

"Your journey here?" Teo grumbled warily. "Not many people intentionally seek out my village. Is there a reason you're here?"

"Yes, we're looking for our friend Kane," explained Gabriel. "Kane Keahi?"

"Kane Keahi." Teo contemplated, staring into nothingness as he sipped his tea.

"I thought his name was Kang Keahi," Selene muttered to Magnolia, which granted her and nudged elbow to her sides.

"I'm not familiar with a Kane Keahi. Could you describe him for me?" Teo requested.

"Where do I start?" Gabriel sighed. "He's kind of tall, dark-skinned, muscular, bold, gruff and angry in demeanour…"

"And a really powerful Kin of Sun," Magnolia added. Gabriel nodded in agreement.

"You say he's a powerful user of his novatus abilities?" Teo asked.

"Yes."

"Then he won't be here."

"Are you sure? Maybe he might have passed by-"

"He *won't* be here." Teo insisted with emphasis.

Teo's blunt disposition confused Gabriel. He could sense that he must have said something wrong, but could not figure out what exactly.

Teo stood up from his seat, intimidating the three with his broad size and stern face. Using his Kin of Land powers, he formed a hole in the earth walls behind them, creating a window peering outside of the house. The trio looked out of the window to see members of the general village going about their day. Some fetched water from a well. Some helped sweep and clean the cobbled streets. Some were playing games with and telling stories to each other in gathered circles. All went about their day in a slow but sure manner.

"When you look across my village, what do you see?" Teo asked, gruff in tone.

"People going about their lives?" Magnolia answered reluctantly.

Teo nodded. "Do you see anyone using their novatus abilities? Do you see anybody fighting? Do you see anybody putting themselves in danger?"

"Uh, no," Magnolia answered again with reluctance.

"Exactly," Teo said with a bold bluntness.

Gabriel furrowed his eyebrows at him. "I'm not sure I understand what you mean," he said.

Teo planted himself back on his throne firmly. "Though you've only described him briefly I can already tell that your friend Kane would not be welcome here," Teo told them sternly. "If your only purpose here is to find him? Then I'd ask you to make your stay here very brief."

Teo manipulated the hole in the wall he made, stretched it out wide enough for him to exit out of, and formed it back into a small hole again, leaving the trio on his sofa.

"Wow he's rude," Selene scoffed.

"I know right, what was all that about?" said Magnolia.

"I don't know." sighed Gabriel. "But judging on how he's acting, I think it's safe to say that he's not going to help us with the Brew-"

Both Gabriel's train of thought and speech were interrupted by the screeching sound of a yelping animal.

"What the hell was that?" asked Gabriel.

"I don't know. A farm animal being slaughtered maybe? Probably nothing to worry about." Magnolia dismissed. "What were you saying again?"

"I was hoping we could kill two birds with one stone and find some more people in this village whilst we looked for Kane," Gabriel explained. "But after that conversation, something tells me we won't find anyone here to help us make the Brew of-"

Gabriel was once again abruptly interrupted by the screeching animal.

"Seriously, what on Earth is that?"

"Are you ever going to finish that sentence?" mocked Selene.

"Yes! What I'm trying to say is, we're not to find any help for the B"

With blistering speed, a fox dove into the house through the hole in the wall whilst releasing the loudest screech it could muster. The fox landed on the laps of the trio, startling them.

"Oh, my Lord!" Magnolia screeched, throwing the fox on the floor on instinct.

As the fox landed on its feet, it acted with haste. The creature grasped Gabriel's sack of scrolls and maps within its mouth and sprinted out of the front door.

"Hey!" Gabriel shouted. Without hesitation, he sprinted to the house's exit door.

***

Gabriel burst out of the house in search of the fox. He saw the creature had already run through most of the village. He sprinted in hot pursuit of the fox, dodging and weaving the slow villagers as they lethargically went about their days.

Gabriel chased the fox out of the main village, past the farmland, and into the woods. Gabriel panted in desperation as he struggled to keep up with the canine as it bounded from tree to tree.

"That's it," Gabriel grunted. He stopped in his tracks, refusing to run any longer.

He built up a large gust of wind in his hands as he stared the rushing fox down. Hearing the build-up of wind behind it and turning to see the origin, the fox decided to stop running and drop the sack to the floor. Gabriel sighed with relief as he walked up to retrieve his sack. As Gabriel was about to walk over to the sack the fox changed before his eyes.

The orange Canidae creature shape-shifted into a short young woman with dark blackened hair. The fox Gabriel had been chasing, was a Kin of Beasts.

"I'm sorry, but I had to do this, Gabriel." the woman said, her voice soft and plush.

"Have we met before?" Gabriel asked.

"No. I only know your name because I heard Teo mention it," she admitted. "One of the many things I overheard you talking about. As well as the Brew of Tranquillity."

"You're familiar with the Brew of Tranquillity?!" asked Gabriel, surprised as ever.

"Yep. Reading ancient legends is one of my favourite hobbies other than running around like a fox," she said irreverently. "I'm probably familiar with a lot in those scrolls of yours."

"Who *are* you?" Gabriel asked.

"Layla Kitsune." she introduced herself. "The one and only."

"What do you want from me, 'Layla'?" Gabriel asked. "Why did you drag me out here?

Layla huffed under her breath as she parted her hair to the side. "I want you to stop trying to talk about The Brew of Tranquillity," she ordered him. "Especially when you're in the main village."

***

"Where did Gabriel even chase that fox to?" Selene asked as she and Magnolia walked around the circular rows of housing in the village centre.

"I don't know but I hope he catches it. It took the bag our map was in," said Magnolia as her eyes surveyed the cobbled streets and mud homes upon them. "The last thing we need is to get lost on our-"

"Ladies," echoed an incredibly deep and quiet voice from behind them. Magnolia and Selene quickly turned to see Teo had quietly snuck up on them with his arms crossed.

"Mr Sten," Magnolia uttered, a slight shakiness about her. "How can we help you?"

"I wanted to find you, to apologise for my behaviour," said Teo. "And to offer up an explanation as to why I showcased said behaviour."

"There's no need for you to do that Mr. Sten. Truly, it's fine," insisted Magnolia.

"No. I insist," urged Teo.

"Whatever, go ahead then if you want," said Selene nonchalantly, Magnolia giving her the evil eye.

Teo nodded his head slowly. "Following the novatus loss of the Second Great War, I abandoned my comrades and immediately started my work to build this settlement. I created this village with one goal in mind - to make sure, if only a few, that I could stop novatus from killing themselves." he started. He tensed his jaw, giving his face a more brutal look. Magnolia tensed quietly as she listened to him. So far, his explanation seemed to have the potential to keep Selene's usually fleeting attention span satiated.

"I had grown tired of seeing our people fight a futile battle in which we could never conceivably win. Some novatus believe in continuously fighting for the cause until our people are liberated and free to go where we want and do as we please. but I'm not one of them. That's who this village was created for. Not just people too weak to fight back, but people like me, too exhausted mentally and spiritually, to do so." Teo explained. "That's why I was wary of you three, especially when you mentioned your powerful friend. The last thing this village needs is to be roped back into the novatus struggle. I want my people to stay quiet, hidden, and in peace."

"I see," said Magnolia softly. "I understand now."

"Once again, I ask you to forgive me for my rudeness before," Teo said. He bowed to Magnolia who immediately returned the gesture.

"So, Gabriel was right then," Selene said. "We're really not going to get anyone to help us make the Br-"

"Thanks for sharing that with us!" Magnolia interrupted in an upbeat but nervous tone.

Teo Sten bowed his head a final time. Satisfied with that conclusion, he walked away from the pair, heading back down the street he had come from.

As soon as she was sure he was out of earshot, Magnolia looked away from him and shot a glare over to Selene.

"Are you serious?"

"What did I do now?"

"Weren't you listening to anything he said? If he got that annoyed over the mere mention of a group of powerful novatus in his village, what makes you think he'll want to hear about us trying to make the Brew?" Magnolia chastised.

"Oh right," said Selene. "Good thing you stopped me from talking then."

Selene laughed, far more amused with herself than Magnolia who groaned at her. The two returned to searching for Gabriel around the village.

Unbeknownst to them, Sten had stopped his walking through the village. Instead of leaving the area as he had made them believe, he was watching them from afar. The village leader grimaced as he glared directly at the back of their wandering heads.

***

"...that's why, under no circumstances, can you even utter the words 'Brew of Tranquillity' within the confines of Kicen Village," said Layla, finishing off the same explanation Teo had given to the girls to Gabriel as they leaned on trees in the forest.

Gabriel took a moment to process the story, parting his hands through his dreadlocks with an unsatisfied look on his face. "I couldn't disagree more," Gabriel grumbled under his breath.

"Sorry?" Layla asked.

"I couldn't disagree more!" Gabriel shouted with a louder passion. "So what if humans have trampled over our people for decades past and so what if they continue to do so for decades to come?! That's no reason for any of us to give up! If anything, that's the reason why we should keep fighting!"

"What do you expect 'our people' to do?" asked Layla. "How are we to fight back? By starting up another war?"

"No! Another war is the last thing I want!" Gabriel insisted. "I understand how Teo feels, I too am tired of fighting, I too wish for no more bloodshed for us novatus!"

"Then what's your solution?" Layla scoffed with derision.

"You already know my solution! You already know I wish to solve this in another way!" Gabriel exclaimed. "You already know I'm going to make The Brew of Tranquillity!"

Gabriel gritted his teeth and clenched his fists as he stared Layla down. The blank look on Layla's face changed into a cheeky grin.

"What's so funny?" grunted Gabriel.

"You, are like a damn child!" Layla laughed. "You honestly think you and your friends are going to get all the way to the Fourth Kingdom without being killed?"

"I appreciate your concern, but we'll be fine-"

"And newsflash, you guys don't even have enough novatus to complete the ritual anyway!" Layla interrupted with laughter.

"Well newsflash back to you! That's the whole reason I sought out this village in the first place! Remember? To find one of my friends and have him join us!" Gabriel retorted.

"That would still leave you two members short! What, were you planning to pull the other two out of your ass? Or do you have more estranged friends who you can't find running around the First Kingdom?" Layla asked mockingly.

Gabriel ground his teeth together harder, unable to come up with a response. Seeing the frustration on his face, Layla laughed even more, hands on her hips as she chuckled at his expense.

Gabriel stood there and took the mockery. With every passing second, Gabriel lost all energy he had to argue with her. He stepped away from the tree and looked to the ground.

"You know when I first saw you transform, I was delighted. I thought that maybe, just maybe, I had found a novatus who could join us as our Kin of Beasts. Another novatus who might be willing to risk it all for the good of something more." he lamented. Layla's laughter gradually died down as she listened to him. "But instead, it seems that all I've found is yet another novatus with no hope for our people whatsoever."

Gabriel shook his head and looked away from Layla. Her smile faded from her face entirely as she glanced down at him. He was too upset to even look at her, his eyes glazed over with a dull sadness. A tinge of guilt seemed to weigh on Layla. She dropped her shoulders, leaned off of the tree, and walked closer to Gabriel.

"Wunkae Desert, Reckonen Asylum and the Prisoner's Forest."

"Sorry, what?" Gabriel asked.

"Wunkae Desert, Reckonen Asylum, and the Prisoner's Forest. Aside from here, these are the only places you'll find novatus on the First Kingdoms mainland unless he's become a slave for the aristocracy." Layla explained. "This Kin of Sun friend you're trying to find, was he taken as a slave?"

"I don't think so."

"Was he taken as a prisoner then, do you think?"

"Nah, he wouldn't be."

"And you're sure that he's in the First Kingdom at all?"

"He has to be! There's only so far, he could have travelled without a ship!"

"Then he's definitely somewhere around Wunkae Desert," said Layla. "That's where members of the Clan of Caelestis meet."

"What's the Clan of Caelestis?"

"A group of novatus freedom fighters that seems to be growing in size over the past few months. They like to think of themselves as this organised clandestine group of liberators, but really, they're just a bunch of novatus who risk their asses running around killing humans at the request of their megalomaniacal leader," she explained to him. "If he's not been taken as a prisoner, a slave or by The Vyre to be fed to The True One, then your friend is most likely with the Clan."

"The Clan of Caelestis," Gabriel muttered as he rubbed his chin. As he contemplated for a moment, his mood lightened. He finally looked Layla in the eye again.

"Thank you for telling me all that Layla, it was very kind of you."

"Whatever. I just wanted you to stop whining." Layla snarked. Gabriel gave Layla a warm smile. She tried her darndest not to return a smile back, but she could not help it.

"How dare you, Gabriel!" echoed a booming voice from beneath the surface.

Emerging from his hidden spot beneath the Earth, Teo clawed his way up from out of the forest floors. Gabriel and Layla's eyes dart over to Sten, as he reveals himself a few metres away from them, his forehead bulging with veiny fury.

"Oh crap," Layla cursed.

"I heard it! I heard it all! All that nonsense about the Brew of Tranquillity! All that nonsense about fighting back!" Teo raged. "Not only do you violate the sanctity of my settlement, but you do so with a traitor of the village? You disgust me!"

"Traitor of the village?" asked Gabriel.

"If you consider becoming a scholar an act of treachery, then yes I suppose I am," said Layla as she narrowed her eyes at Sten.

"I don't understand," said Gabriel.

"I've already banished you for your crimes! Don't make me do it again!" Teo warned her.

"Sharing knowledge with the people of the village is not a crime."

"Yes, it is! And now I've caught you committing it again."

"How?!"

"By whispering rumours of novatus sightings and rebellions alike!" Teo said in outrage. "We don't need more novatus falling for such foolish causes! Not in Kicen Village!"

"The information I gave him would send him *away* from the village." Kayla insisted. "Once he's gone, who cares what he does with it?!"

"I care!" Teo screamed. "I simply *cannot* stand by and let my people suffer from such delusions!"

Teo manipulated the earth of the forest floor below him. He pulled it out of the ground, raising himself upwards until he stood above the trees on a mountain of stone. Standing atop his makeshift mountain, Teo raised both his hands to the sky. With the twitch of his fingers, Teo called upon every stone in the general vicinity his power could muster to circle him in a cloud of rock.

Gabriel and Layla watched as Teo Sten's Kin of Land abilities whittled down every stone into hundreds of sharp blades that rained down on their heads, ready to cut them to pieces.

SAY MY FULL NAME

Gabriel grabbed Layla with him as he flew to the side. The two landed back on the floor, narrowly avoiding Teo's raining stone blades as they pierced the ground.

"Yes, that's right! Kick off! Show your true colours!" Layla shouted, goading him. "A petty man who withholds knowledge and information from his people and tries to kill those who want anything more!"

"QUIET TRAITOR!" Teo bellowed with a powerful ferocity.

Gabriel and Layla stood at the ready, their eyes fixed on Teo as he raised his hands to the sky. The ground beneath them shook and rocks protruded out of the earth with spiked attacks from below. Morphing into her fox form, Layla sprinted across the floor, using her powerful jaw to bite away every chunk of stone as it came up.

Gabriel's fingers crackled with lightning as he hovered above Layla and the rocks. With a swing of his arms, he unleashed a barrage of bolts toward Teo. Teo consumed each lightning shot using flying clumps of mud. He compiled these mucky projectiles and sent them flying back in retaliation. Gabriel dodged one, then two, then three clumps of lightning-enhanced mud, but was too slow to avoid a fifth, sixth, seventh, and eighth, sending him back down to the ground.

Fox Layla bounded across the forest at inhuman speeds, drool dripping from her gaping jaw as she charged to Sten. She leaped onto a nearby tree, then bounded off it for momentum as she flung herself towards him, ready to bite. Her attack was stopped dead in its tracks with an earth wall coming up from the ground, knocking her out of the air.

As Teo smirked down at Layla, Gabriel attempted to get the drop on him, sprinting towards him with a charged-up air cyclone in the palm of his hands. Teo was quick to react.

He coated his face in a thick rocky surface, negating the impact of the cyclone as Gabriel punched him. With a foot coated in rock, he kicked Gabriel in the chest, sending him rolling on the floor, back where he came from. He clutched at his chest in deep pain.

Teo turned his attention away from Gabriel just in time to see Fox Layla lunging at his leg. He could not coat his leg in rock in time, allowing her to sink teeth into the skin above his ankle and draw blood. Teo grunted in pain as he thrashed to release his leg from her jaws. Coating an arm in a substance extremely sharp to the touch, he drove it downwards. His rocky elbow stabbed Layla in the back so hard he not only forced her to let go of his leg but to transform back into her human form. She plunged to the floor, wincing in agony.

"Crap! Layla!" Gabriel grunted, still winded from his blows.

She lay there, dazed, and battered, her body aching from the impact.

Teo strolled towards her, his eyes glinting with malice. With a raise of his hand, a cloud of dust rose around him. When the dust cleared, he stood before Layla, a sharp blade of stone having formed in the palm of his hand.

"This is the end for you, traitor," he said, his voice cold and menacing.

Layla closed her eyes, waiting for the blow to come. But it never did.

Chunks of Earth protruded from the ground, beating Teo in the face and preventing him from finishing her off. For a moment, it seemed to them like Teo Sten had made a foolish error and attacked himself with his own abilities. That was until they saw Magnolia and Selene rushing into the forest, jumping to their aid without hesitation.

"What do you two think you're doing?!" Sten roared at them.

"Unaccepting your apology," mocked Selene. Out of the palm of her hands, Selene generated two whips out of dark energy and slashed Teo across the face, knocking him out of the way and into a tree.

"Who's this Gabriel?" Magnolia asked warily as she gestured at Layla.

"Layla. She's a Kin of Beast," Gabriel explained as he walked over to the rest of them. "Don't worry, she's with us, not *him*."

"Any friend of Gabriel's is a friend of mine," Selene said irreverently.

"Thanks, I guess," Layla grunted in deep pain as the girls helped her to her feet.

"*Friends* of Gabriel." scoffed Teo as he too got back up. "You shall all die together as *traitors* of the village!"

The four braced themselves as Teo charged back into action. The second he was within striking range, they attacked him at once with the full force of their power. Gabriel summoned a powerful gust of wind and struck Teo with lightning. Layla transformed into a fox and pounced on him; her sharp claws extended. Combining the moisture from the forest floor with her shadow manipulation powers, Selene slammed him with a massive wave of dark water. Magnolia created a collection of twisting vines and sharp thorns that ensnared him and pierced into his skin.

With fists of rocks, Sten punched outwards knocking all of the attacks off of him. His gyrating hands brought a dozen rock pillars out of the ground and flung them in all directions. Selene summoned a shield of dark water to protect herself, but the projectile shattered it with ease and knocked her to the ground. Gabriel managed to deflect a few with clouds of wind yet others struck him with painful force. Magnolia summoned a wall of earth to shield herself, but it was quickly worn away by the onslaught. Layla tried to leap out of the way, though found she was too late and promptly knocked to the ground with the rest of them.

Sten pressed his advantage, as Gabriel and Magnolia tried to climb back up again. He conjured rippling waves of mud and earth that swept the group off their feet. He followed with an instant blast of pure kinetic force that sent them tumbling even further.

Selene struggled back up to her feet and brought open a trilogy of dark energy whips to lash out at Sten once more. He was too quick, ducking and weaving out of their whipping range, then striking her with a sharp blow from a flying rock that left her gasping for air.

Magnolia summoned vines from the ground to ensnare Sten, only for him to shatter them with a burst of raw power from his rock-coated muscles. Gabriel created a swirling tornado to lift him into the air, but Sten merely laughed, summoning a wave of earth to ground himself. With a wave of his hand, he sent a boulder hurtling at Gabriel, striking him in the chest so hard that he fell to the floor coughing up blood.

Teo wasted no time. Magnolia, Selene, and Layla all received the matching boulder attacks hurtling them to the ground. One, two, and three. Sten's earthly attacks resigned them to curled-up balls of pain on the floor, wheezing, and coughing up blood. To further seal his victory, Sten rained sharp pebbles, belting down on the bodies of the four before they could even think of rising again. He scoffed down at quartet laying there, too battered and bruised to face him any longer.

In one swift action, Sten shifted the earth to propel Layla's barely conscious body to him and sent the sack of scrolls and maps to Gabriel. With Layla in his hands and the sack landing on Gabriel's stomach, Teo scoffed at the injured trio again.

"Let those wounds act as a lesson to you," he said. "Leave my village and never return!"

Teo slung Layla over his shoulder and marched away from the trio.

"Get back here Sten!" Gabriel shouted at him. "GET BACK-"

Gabriel's screams were drowned out by the sounds of the crackling earth that gave way beneath them. Those familiar mud walls closed in over them and they were plunged back into subterranean depths of darkness.

A few seconds passed and the mud walls that encapsulated the trio sank back into the ground. The darkness cleared and the trio were back in the field of yellow grass, with Kicen Village nowhere to be seen. Magnolia and Selene curled up on the floor, still clutching their wounded bodies, too tired to get up. Gabriel however, threw the sack of scrolls off of his stomach and leaped back up to his feet.

"STEEEEN!" Gabriel screamed at the top of his lungs in frustration, his voice echoing through the empty field.

***

Grand Leader Franz Kaymore of the First Kingdom was known to be a man of excess. Since the celebratory banquet he had in honour of Nathanael Reyan, he had hosted two more needless banquets and was in the middle of hosting a third.

As usual, Kaymore sat at the head of the long table of jovial jewellery-obsessed aristocrats in the dining room as they ate, drank, and were merry.

Unlike the previous banquets, the slaves had already been brought out by the knight's guard ahead of time. As per routine, the aristocrats threw food, drink, and verbal mockery at the slaves. Though this time, the knight-guards were not in the room and had left the chained slaves to the complete mercy of the aristocracy. As 'Kaymore's favourite' Enzo was the slave that received the brunt of the abuse, with Kaymore parading him about at the head of the table.

"Look at this!" Kaymore laughed as he picked up a steak and threw it at Enzo. The greasy slab of meat slammed against his face, staining his cheek as it dropped down to the floor. "You see that? They let you do anything to them!"

Kaymore's aristocratic comrades erupted into a chorus of belly laughter. Some took turns in throwing their steaks at the chained slaves, mostly targeting Enzo. The slave clenched his jaw tight, wincing as he forced himself not to cry.

The cruel aristocrats had their fun interrupted by a rampant banging so forceful it could have knocked the door down.

"Who is that?! What do you want?!" Kaymore shouted. Silence followed.

Kaymore sighed. "Go on, come in then! We've not got all day!"

All eyes were on the dining room door, impatiently waiting for it to finally open. When it did, the individual who was beating at the door did not enter. A rolling decapitated head engulfed in flames, entered in their place.

The aristocratic guests gasped as the burning severed head rolled across the floor, stopping right at their table. They had no time to even process the shock of the first one with a second, third, and fourth set of burning decapitated heads rolling into the room right after. Kaymore's face lost its colour as he recognised the faces of the heads that burnt on his palace floor. The air was thick with the scent of smoke and the stench of burning flesh as the heads of Kaymore's knight-guards continued to roll in.

The room erupted into chaos as the door suddenly burst open and a horde of Clan of Caelestis members poured in, wielding their novatus abilities with no caution whatsoever.

One of them lifted her hand and sent an ice pick hurtling through the air, piercing through the head of an aristocrat, killing him instantly. Another member of the Clan focused their powers on a large stone block embedded in the wall, which they promptly ripped from its perch and sent hurtling through the air, crushing another aristocrat's head, his flesh and skull flattening with a sickly crunch.

Not wanting them to take up all the fun, Kane made his way to the front of the group of clan members. He rubbed his hands together in malevolent glee and conjured a ball of searing flames, hurling it at a third aristocrat. The man's screams were deafening as the flames quickly consumed him.

Any peace and joy that the room of aristocrats once held had been eviscerated. The clan members ran around the dining room as they chased the aristocrats who attempted to flee. The Clan members who did not focus on killing aristocrats, focused their efforts on breaking the chains that bound all of the slaves. Apart from one.

Quivering with fear, Kaymore pulled Enzo in front of him and cowered behind him.

"Help me Enzo!" he cried.

"How?!" Enzo asked in a panic.

"I don't know! Just do something!" Kaymore pleaded.

Enzo watched as the Clan of Caelestis cut, burnt, electrocuted, and slashed the aristocrats to pieces. Confusion and uncertainty rang through his body and showed on his face. Though this did not last for very long. He slowly but surely sported a wicked smile that stretched its way across his face. With his wicked smile reaching its crazed apex, he turned around to flash it at Kaymore.

"Enzo?" Kaymore uttered in confusion.

"Enzo what?" Enzo snapped to him. The entire makeup of his personality had changed within an instant. From timid and meek-voiced to cocky and baritone. "Say my full name,"

Kaymore stumbled backwards from Enzo, falling back onto his chair. He stared up at his former slave, at a complete loss for words. Enzo laughed.

"Oh, that's right. You don't know it," he chuckled. "Well let me inform you."

Enzo held out his chained hands in front of his face. A lightning bolt sent down from the heavens, broke through the many floors of Kaymore's Castle to strike these chains and break him free. Franz Kaymore watched on in silent shocked horror as Enzo stretched his arms out. With the gusts of wind that formed around him and the clan burning the dining room behind him, Enzo looked the role of a heavenly demon before his very eyes.

"I am Enzo Caelestis! Leader of Clan Caelestis!" Enzo shouted down at Kaymore with pride. "The man who will bring down The First Kingdom!".

WUNKAE DESERT

"So, we're just going to leave your friend Layla there with Sten?" asked Magnolia. Her face was plagued with concern and speckled with sweat as she walked alongside Gabriel and Selene through Wunkae Desert. A couple of days had passed since their fight with Sten. Their injuries from it had only just about healed up the evening prior. Nonetheless, with bags on their backs and water canisters in their hands, they carried on their journey with purpose and determination.

"You heard him. I have no doubt that if we ever stepped back in the village, he'd kill us," said Gabriel, his eyes squinting as the sun beat down on him. "And it's not like we could find it again anyway."

"I don't know if I'd *want* to even try it again. That earth crap he used to transport us in and out hurt like a bitch!" said Selene.

"Yeah, you guys are right," sighed Magnolia.

"Maybe one day, when we're stronger, we can go back and save her," Gabriel suggested. "But for now, all we can do is make sure that the information she gave me doesn't go to waste."

"That information might have just been a load of bull-crap," said Selene, kicking the reddish sand beneath her with each step she took. "There's like, nothing here."

Selene's assessment was correct. The closest things to signs of other life the trio had seen since they had entered the desert were the tattered strips of abandoned tents and skeletal structures of rotted animals. It was as if they were in the fields of yellow grass all over again, only hotter, and harder to slog through.

"Trust me, we'll find Kane and the clan somewhere around here," assured Gabriel.

"How are we going to find this 'Clan of Caelestis'?" asked Magnolia.

Selene glanced over at her with a mischievous look in her eyes. Magnolia shook her head, immediately realising what she was about to do.

"CLAN OF CAELESTIS! CLAN OF CAELESTIS! CLAN OF CAELESTIS!" Selene shouted. "WE'RE LOOKING FOR THE CLAN OF CAELESTIS!"

"Shut up Selene! That's not going to do anything!" Gabriel exclaimed, Selene giggling at his irritation. "It's ridiculous that it even worked the first time, it's not going to work a second-"

A flurry of swirling sand generated around the three in circles, thickening and clouding their vision. The three watched as the sand condensed itself into a thick moving marriage that swarmed them. A series of figures started to emerge from within the sand. Silhouettes of young men and women appeared around them. Though their identities were covered by the clouds of sand, one thing was clear - a couple of members of the Clan of Caelestis had come to visit.

"You can't be serious," Magnolia groaned. Selene burst into another fit of laughter which was abruptly stopped by a coughing fit brought on by the sand.

"You hear that guys? They're looking for the Clan of Caelestis," growled one of the clan members hidden in the sand. His comrades chuckled alongside him in an intimidating circle of synchronised laughter. Gabriel and Magnolia's eyes darted around as the members sprinted around and enclosed them in sand.

"Really? They don't look too pleased to see us?" laughed another member.

"Maybe they don't want to see us anymore?" laughed the first voice.

"Then they should be careful what they wish for!" shrieked another one of the clan members. Upon her call, the hidden figures manipulated the sand around them and formed it into four thick brick walls moving inwards. Rock-hard spears made of pure sand jutted out of the walls and closed in for the kill. As the spikes approached, Gabriel frantically generated a cyclone within his hands. Having no time to direct it at anyone in particular, he let it grow and expand outwards. The cyclone burst in an explosive gust of air, powerful enough to blow all four walls down and knock everyone but Gabriel to their feet. The explosion filled the area with specks of sand.

Magnolia and Selene rose up again as Gabriel used the wind to clear the air. The trio saw the ten members of the Clan of Caelestis that had surrounded them, standing in a circle no longer hidden by the sand. One of the members, a handsome man with crooked teeth, flashed his broken smile at Gabriel.

"Ohhhh, you're novatus aren't you?" he asked.

"Yeah, we are," Magnolia said, her voice laced with a hint of vexation.

"Our mistake. Welcome to the desert friends," said a woman with bleached orange hair.

"Thank you, friends," Selene said with a nonchalant nod

"So that's why you were looking for us. Looking to join, are you?"

"Yes," Gabriel answered, a reluctance about him.

The Clan of Caelestis smirked at the trio, eyeing up their 'fresh meat.'

"Have you brought a Vyre head offering in one of those sacks?" asked the handsome crooked man.

"Nope. Sorry friends," Selene said.

The clan members shared wary looks with one another, stared at the trio in disappointment then glanced back at each other again. Gabriel, Magnolia, and Selene waited with bated breath as the clan had their non-verbal conversation.

The handsome crooked man guffawed at them. "You're lucky you came at the right time, friends."

"What does that mean?" asked Gabriel.

"Usually, we'd only let fresh faces in if they gave us a Vyre head offering first and foremost," the handsome crook explained. "But considering the move our leader recently made, we could use the extra numbers."

"Brilliant!" cheered Selene, much to the handsome crook's amusement.

Gabriel nodded in understanding as he made eye contact with him whilst Magnolia made efforts to avoid his uncomfortable gaze.

The crooked-toothed man smiled as the other members laughed behind him. "Welcome to the Clan of Caelestis friends."

***

The walls were scorched with fire and singed with lightning, turning the stone from white to grey. Every piece of fine furniture or cutlery within the room had been destroyed. Instead of aristocrats dancing around a large dining table, novatus clan members stomped around the empty floor space in wicked celebration. The dining palace of the First Kingdoms Grand Castle had been well and truly turned into Enzo Caelestis' playpen.

Enzo stood at the back of the room, all eyes on him as he climbed atop Kaymore's head of the table chair, the only item in the room they had not destroyed. He stood upon the chair and waved his hands about to get the attention of all the people in the room. The rampant rushing around of the clan members subsided as they looked to their leader. With their attention grasped, Enzo pointed towards the ceiling. His hands crackled with lightning as he raised them higher. He closed his fist emphatically.

Moments after Enzo closed his fist, the sounds of Franz Kaymore's electrocuted screams from several floors above could be faintly heard.

Enzo and the clan laughed incessantly. "Apologies for the noise, people. My *slave* is still getting accustomed to his new room." he joked. The clan laughed as if he had made the funniest quip of the century.

He jumped down from his position atop the chair and sat firmly in it. He reclined into the wooden throne, all eyes in the room still fixated on him.

Enzo smirked. "How fortunate am I?" he beamed as he surveyed his eyes over the room of novatus. "How many people can say that they have a group of beautiful, healthy, and capable young novatus willing to fight for their cause!"

"Not many! Not many at all!" shouted the voice of a woman from the crowd, much to the rest of the clan's jubilation. Enzo leaped back on top of the chair.

"Right!" he shouted. "And that's why soon, us novatus shall take over this Kingdom!"

The room was drowned out with the thunderous sounds of rounds of applause as Enzo swirled storm clouds around himself. Deep within the thick of the clan's crowd, Kane was there, giving Enzo the biggest round of applause of them all. A sparkle of light shone in his eyes as he clapped his hands together so hard, it caused his Kin of Sun abilities to generate smoke from between his palms. As Enzo's eyes surveyed the clan crowd, he immediately took notice of Kane and the smoke his applause generated. Enzo winked at Kane, filling the young novatus with immense amounts of pride.

***

Kane took the pride he felt when Enzo noticed him and channelled it into something greater. Deep within the rocky rooms on the underground floor of the Grand Castle, the Clan of Caelestis had repurposed the barren dungeons into a training area.

In one of these dungeons, Kane trained alongside a male Kin of Moon and a female Kin of Man. Together, the three of them stood on one side of the dungeon across from the dozens of corpses of Kaymore's knight-guards which were nailed to the wall on the other side. The Kin of Moon used water-based projectiles to hit a few of the corpses accurately. The Kin of Man used throwing-knives to hit most of the corpses accurately. Both of them were no match for Kane who used balls of light energy to hit the bullseye on every single corpse head.

The three clan members' training session was interrupted by the creaking of a wooden door.

"Kane?" a woman called as she peered her head through the door.

"Yes?"

"There's some new clan members here. They want to see you specifically."

Kane's eyebrows furrowed as he marched his way over to the door. He arrived by the room's exit, the woman opening the door further to show his visitors. Standing there, Kane saw Gabriel, Magnolia, and Selene, all waiting for him.

"You know these people?" asked the woman.

"Yes…" said Kane, a small smile forming at the corner of his mouth. "They're old shelter-mates of mine."

Kane observed the trio measuredly. He smiled at Magnolia who awkwardly smiled back at him. He raised an eyebrow at Selene, clearly not recognising her. She smiled and waved at him as if he did and he rolled his eyes, choosing to ignore her. Finally, he focused his attention solely on Gabriel.

"Hello Gabriel," Kane greeted.

"Hello Kane," he greeted back.

CLEANSING

The people of the First Kingdoms mainland were in a state of panic and disarray. Not only had their Grand Leader's castle been sacked and knight-guards killed, but they had been plagued with increasing numbers of novatus' making themselves known, pillaging their villages, and taking their towns. The Clan of Caelestis' influence was quickly spreading. The humans of the First Kingdom begged and prayed for Reyan, The Vyre, or any outside force to come back to put these novatus in their place. Thus far, no outside force had arrived, and Reyan and his Vyre soldiers were not coming to their aid anytime soon.

Reyan and hundreds of his soldiers had taken a grand fleet and sailed out to the high seas of the outer Kingdom. Reyan stood by the helm on the top deck of the superhumanly large and equally fast beast of a ship as they tore through the ocean. He steered the ship with only one hand, his other hand being occupied with a strange clump of flesh and fur. Fur that was a similar colour to that of the True One's otherworldly coating.

***

Gabriel, Selene, and Magnolia entered a small dark dungeon room followed by Kane who shut the door behind them. As the trio settled into the tight enclosure, Kane leant on the back of the door with his arms folded and eyes narrowed.

"Of all the novatus that could've joined, you two are the last ones I expected to see here," Kane said as he lasered in on Gabriel and Magnolia. "Especially you, Gabriel. Don't tell me I gifted you that spot on the rescue mission for nothing?"

"There *is* no rescue mission anymore," Magnolia informed him.

"Why not?" Kane asked.

"Because all the prisoners of war were killed."

The words had barely left her mouth and Kane was already flushed with fury upon hearing them. "What the hell?! When did this happen?!"

"A couple of weeks after you disappeared without telling anyone," Gabriel said with condemnation. "The same day The Vyre came to the Peninsula and killed most of the Protectors."

The news shook Kane to his core, his teeth grinding and eyes flared. "The Vyre attacked the shelter?"

"Yes. Reyan even came and killed most of the Protectors himself," lamented Magnolia.

"And Dillon…" Gabriel added quietly, Magnolia resting a sympathetic hand on his shoulder. A vein in Kane's neck bulged with righteous anger.

"What are you doing here then?! Why aren't you protecting the shelter in case they return?!" Kane chastised.

"We could ask you the same thing with the original mission!" Gabriel shouted back at him. "Why would you leave the shelter at such an important time? For *here* of all places?!"

"What I'm doing here with the clan will work to accomplish the protection of all of novatus kind, not just the shelter," Kane retorted. "So, I think you can forgive me for leaving."

"Well, *we're* doing will do a much better job at doing that than your stupid clan thingies!" Selene added, feeling left out of the conversation.

Kane glared at her through the corner of his eye. "What exactly is *she* talking about?" he asked the other two as he pointed at her. Gabriel and Magnolia glanced over at each other briefly. They both looked as if they had something to say but neither of them wanted to say it. Looks that visibly frustrated Kane. Finally, Gabriel stepped up.

"Kane. Are you familiar with the story of the novatus who secreted his powers in a special lake that calmed the True One when it drank its water?" asked Gabriel.

"Are you talking about The Brew of Tranquillity?" Kane asked, his eyes lighting up.

"Yes! The Brew of Tranquillity!" Magnolia confirmed excitedly.

"Yeah, I vaguely recall hearing that story from time to time," Kane answered warily. "Why?"

"Well, we're going to try and make it. Me as the Kin of Skies, Magnolia as the Kin of Land and Selene as the Kin of Moon." Gabriel explained. "And that's why we're here. We want you to join us, as the Kin of Sun."

Kane stared at him blankly as he let the information settle. The trio stared back, waiting on his response. That signature corner of the mouth smirk made its way upon Kane's face.

"That's why you came all the way here to find me? To rope me into your fairy-tail mission?" Kane derided.

"What are you talking about, there were no fairies in that tale," said Selene. Kane rolled his eyes at her and scoffed again.

"It may not sound like a plausible plan, but it's worth the try." Magnolia insisted.

"It's ridiculous, that's what it is." scoffed Kane.

"You're not the first person to tell me that and you won't be the last," Gabriel said. "Regardless, I've made up my mind and they're willing to go with me."

Magnolia and Selene nodded in corroboration with him. Kane's face twisted at them in disbelief.

"You know Gabriel, you've always been an over-idealistic stupid bastard, but this really takes the cake!" Kane mocked.

Gabriel scowled at Kane. With the look on his face and the tone of his voice, Gabriel could not tell whether Kane was more amused or annoyed by him.

"If you actually want to make a difference for novatus kind, disregard that Brew crap and help us out here at the clan," suggested Kane. "Caelestis is going to bring our people to glory and the First Kingdom down to its knees."

"No. That's *not* the right way to do things,"

"And why's that?"

"Because it will only add another link to the chain of never-ending violence! Making the Brew is the only way to save our people without condemning them to further retaliation from humans!" Gabriel explained. "We can't afford to let the chain go on."

Kane paused for a second. For a brief while, he seemed as if he was contemplating Gabriel's philosophy and considering its validity. That quickly proved to not be the case.

"My lord, you are a fucking dumbass!" Kane erupted in laughter. Gabriel let out a deep frustrated sigh from his flared nostrils. Magnolia and Selene could see that his patience was quickly running thin.

"Don't be like that, Kane," pleaded Magnolia. "The least you could do is show some respect. We travelled all this way just to ask you."

"Well then you wasted your time." scoffed Kane. "Unless you're planning on staying with the clan, you better travel all the way back."

Kane soon left the room, slamming the door behind him. He left the trio there to stew in their frustration, Gabriel most of all.

"Oh well, we tried," shrugged off Selene. "So where should we go next-"

"NO!" Gabriel interrupted with emphatic emphasis. "He *will* join us. I'm going to make sure of it..."

***

Later that day, almost all of the members of the Clan of Caelestis gathered together in a tightly knit crowd. They filled the dining palace with some spilling out into the red-carpeted halls past the swung open door. Hundreds of novatus were cramped together as they looked towards Enzo, who stood at the back of the room, speaking in front of them on the throne again. Kane was at the very front of this crowd, hanging onto every word Enzo made in his speech. Gabriel, Selene, and Magnolia stood within the back of the crowd closer to the red-carpet halls than to Enzo's wooden throne. Unlike the other members, Gabriel was not completely encapsulated by Enzo, with half of his attention focused on the back of Kane's head.

125

"...and once we're done with conquering The First Kingdom, we'll conquer the Second, the Third and the Fourth!" Enzo shouted as he continued another one of his passionate speeches. "Then, when we've conquered all four kingdoms, we'll kill the True One, expand our powers and collectively take his place as the builders of the world!"

Enzo ended his speech by generating booming thunderclouds around to emphasise his triumph. The booming sound of the thunder he formed was still no match for the loud cheers of the Clan as a whole who celebrated his sentiments for minutes on end in as noisily raucous of fashion as they could.

"Woah, this guy's ambitious," Selene commented as the crowd quietened down.

"Ambitiously insane." Magnolia scoffed. "He's not serious about replacing the True One as the builder of the world, is he?"

Gabriel studied Enzo from afar, seeing the megalomaniacal fervour in his eyes. "I think he is," he answered.

"Now, it's time we got back to work," Enzo added. "This land isn't going to cleanse itself of humans."

With a roaring chant to shake the room once more, the Clan of Caelestis were ready to carry out their leaders' wishes. Gabriel was the least moved by Enzo's words, his attention still glued to Kane.

***

In squads of twenty, the Clan of Caelestis ran through the towns of the First Kingdoms mainland, their elemental powers wreaking havoc, terrorising, and killing the humans who lived there. Enzo led the charge, using fists full of grey winds and bolts of pure lightning to strike down crowds and landmarks alike. The rest of the Clan followed, each using their elemental powers to expand their reign of chaos.

Kane fought with vigour, his fire and light energy burning and blinding any humans who dared to stand in his way. He moved with agility and perspicacity as he burnt down rows of fleeing victims that passed him by.

Gabriel and Magnolia were not as keen on the rampant killing of the fleeing humans as Kane was. Gabriel mostly used his winds to knock down humans whilst Magnolia entangled them in vines. Some members of the clan noticed this and were wary of their apprehension.

Selene had fewer qualms than the other two in this regard yet irritated the clan even more in another way. Reckless with the use of her abilities, she laughed maniacally, summoning dark energy from the shadows and water from the wells to attack the townspeople. With how powerful and unrefined her abilities were, it was often the case that the other clan members would be hit as often as humans were.

Throughout the mission, Kane struggled to hide the second-hand embarrassment he received as the clan members condemned the trio for the way each of them fought. Whilst he made conscious efforts to avoid Gabriel and co., they were futile, as Gabriel made efforts to stick by his side.

"Following me around like a dog isn't going to make me change my mind about your goddamn Brew mission," Kane grunted at him in the middle of one of their battles.

"Randomly killing townspeople isn't going to stop generations of novatus trauma," Gabriel retorted.

"You've lost me," Kane scoffed at Gabriel. Blasting fire from the palm of his hands, he flew away.

As they pieced through the towns, Enzo gave orders to his Clan members, directing them to specific targets and areas. Any humans who made efforts to fight back were quickly overwhelmed by the power of the clan. Without the aristocracy, the knight-guards or the Vyre to save them, the townspeople had their streets littered with bodies and rubble.

After hours of carnage, the Clan of Caelestis stopped in the centre of the town. Enzo raised his arms, the thunderclouds above crackling with energy, and let out a triumphant roar. The rest of the clan cheered, revelling in the utter destruction they had just caused.

***

In the evening, the Clan returned to the dining palace and for the first time since Enzo had sacked the castle, they used it for what it was intended for. The area was rife with celebration, not a single novatus' hand being free of a clump of meat and a mug of beer.

"Here's to today!" Enzo cheered as he threw a cup of ale in the air. "And let tomorrow be a day of human cleansing, just as successful as this one! Cheers!"

"CHEERS!" the crowd shouted back with passion.

Selene enjoyed the party without a care in the world, singing and dancing with the other clan members whilst using her liquid manipulation powers to pour alcohol from multiple people's mugs into her mouth. Magnolia was not having as good of a time, struggling to entertain the many young men who tried their hand at flirting with her. Meanwhile, Gabriel did not interact with anyone. He spent his time sifting his way through the crowd in the room, looking for someone in particular.

"This is fun," Gabriel commented, nodding, and smiling as he approached Kane.

Sipping a drink on his own in the corner of the room, Kane shook his head at Gabriel with disappointment.

"Is this your thinly veiled and poorly constructed way of starting a conversation so you can pivot it towards influencing me to join you again?" Kane deduced.

Gabriel sighed in defeat. "Might as well skip straight to the point then," he said. "Kane, I think you're making a mistake by involving yourself with this clan."

"And I think you're making an even bigger mistake with your horrendously braindead Brew of Tranquillity idea."

"Fair enough," Gabriel sighed. "But I wonder, will you hold the same when the humans finally retaliate and tear this Caelestis Clan to the ground?"

Kane paused in the middle of a sip of beer. He looked Gabriel dead in the eyes with menace. "Don't jinx it now, *Gabriel.*" he quipped. Once again, he sounded both humoured and greatly irritated by Gabriel.

"I'm just being honest. This clan stuff is not going to last. It's unrealistic to think it will."

"The boy who wants to create The Brew of Tranquillity is talking about realism?"

"I'm telling you Kane, the second Reyan and The Vyre step foot in the First Kingdom, you, Enzo and the rest of us are done for."

"I highly doubt that."

"Well, you shouldn't."

"We have the strength to fight back if they do."

"They have the numbers to flatten you if they do."

"Who knew Gabriel Elijah could have such little fate in the will of his people?"

"Who knew Kane Keahi could be so naive?"

Following their verbal sparring match, Gabriel and Kane glared at each other. The two novatus stared each other down with intensity. Tension filled the air to the point where it would be no surprise if either of them violently struck the other.

"I know you want to believe otherwise, but Enzo is not the man who is going to solve our people's problems," Gabriel affirmed. "He's not the type of leader us novatus need to usher us into a new age."

"And you are?" Kane scorned.

"That's not what I'm saying," said Gabriel.

"Sounds like it is," Kane derided. The two engaged in another glaring contest as Gabriel struggled to come up with a response. Kane scoffed at Gabriel and walked away.

Once again, Gabriel found himself stewing in frustration after having failed to convince Kane of anything. He hung his head, the sound of the clan's celebrations echoing behind him.

***

The very image of a fall from grace, Grand Leader Franz Kaymore of the First Kingdom was chained to the wall of the room that was once Enzo's to dwell in as a slave.

The captured royal grovelled on the floors of his stone cell. His previously pristine robes had been soiled with his own urine and faecal matter and his previously clear skin was now scarred and burnt from Enzo's electrocutions. With not much to do, Franz spent his nights in his cell sleepless. He whimpered to himself quietly from dusk till dawn as the Clan of Caelestis used his castle as a novatus hub for hedonism and violence.

That night, Franz's whimpering session was interrupted. A flaming arrow flew through his window and landed inches away from his foot, startling him upwards.

Kaymore turned his head quickly, his eyes darting out of the window. Several feet below him he saw two men standing on the outer grass fields. Both men wore damaged armour and suffered from cuts, bruises and burn scars on their faces. He was looking at the only other survivors of the night Enzo and the clan had sacked the castle during the banquet.

Franz's jaw dropped, surprised to see that any of his guards were alive. The guards looked up at Franz's castle cell window, disgusted by what had been done to their king and determined to undo it.

BATTLE AT THE CASTLE OF DEBRIS

As the morning light began to filter through the windows, Selene's babbling had reached a new level. Her words were slurred and unintelligible as she stumbled around, barely able to keep herself upright. Gabriel and Magnolia took turns supporting her, trying to keep her in one place. A difficult task. She giggled uncontrollably, swaying from side to side, and nearly fell to the ground several times.

Despite the time, the heavy partying continued. Novatus sang songs and danced, while Enzo regaled them with tales of their heroic feats from the previous night. The air was thick with the smell of alcohol and sweat, and the noise was deafening. Even as the celebrations began to wind down, many of the clan members were either too tired or too intoxicated to join in.

Kane sat back in his corner, motionless, with an empty mug of beer in his hand. The events from the previous night had left him drained and in need of rest. His eyes were half-closed, and his breathing was slow and steady. He was all but ready to drift off to sleep.

As Enzo and the clan dragged on their loud celebrations, the door to the dining palace was violently banged upon. The first initial pounds of the door were ignored but as the banging continued, more of the novatus were pulled away from their revelry. The sounds of explosions echoed faintly in the background as the banging persisted. The formerly hard-partying Clan of Caelestis ground their celebrations to a halt. The sixty or so of them who had not already passed out from drinking or fallen asleep, were encapsulated by the banging on the door and faint explosions behind it.

Enzo stood up warily, charging his hands with lightning in preparation. His eyes scoured across the room as he quietly advised the clan members to stay on guard. The members obliged, especially Gabriel who urged Magnolia and Selene to do the same. Even the drunken Selene, who although struggling to stand up straight, clenched her fists in preparation for a fight.

Kane was the readiest of them all, shooting up from his space in the corner and bolting closer to the middle of the palace where most of the novatus were congregating.

The banging intensified, not just on the door, but on the walls surrounding the palace. Without warning, the door and walls suddenly burst open and broke down. Rubble and smoke filled the area as cannon balls shot through the air and caved in the ceiling.

Amidst the debris and chaos, a legion of knight-guards dressed in golden armour and weaponry emerged. Stood in a tight formation, hundreds strong, they surrounded a large cannon. The proud golden knights stood together with broad shoulders and stern faces. Slung over said broad shoulders, were the bodies of the Caelestis Clan members who were supposed to be guarding the rest of the castle.

Enzo clenched his lightning-charged fists in anger. His face was marked with beading sweat and disbelief, both of which only grew as he looked to the back of the legion.

Directing the golden warriors, was a freed Franz Kaymore who stood on the shoulders of two burly knights. The sight of him alone had the entire clan sharing their leader's disbelief. Franz had managed to escape his captivity and had brought with him a formidable army.

The knights picked Franz off of their shoulders and delicately placed him down on the floor, a decent chunk of the legion parting ways to showcase their Grand Leader in all his glory.

"You were a fool for thinking you could turn the tables," Kaymore mocked. "I was never going to stay locked up for long."

Enzo's forehead vein pulsed with fury as he migrated to the middle of the clan army crowd, mirroring Kaymore's position. The novatus clan held silent in disbelief. Gabriel looked over towards Kane and gave him an 'I told you so' look. Kane gritted his teeth as he made his way to the front of the novatus army, only metres away from the golden human knights and the smarmy ruler who brought them.

"Thought just by killing legions of my men you could conquer my land, did you?" asked Kaymore mockingly. "Well, you thought wrong. Because in the Royal Kaymore Family of the First Kingdom - the only thing deeper than our pockets are our armies!"

He laughed maniacally as his men unsheathed their golden swords, spears, and maces.

Enzo closed his eyes and took a deep breath, determined not to let the situation rattle him. He calmly opened his eyes again, with a new look of passion and vigour.

"Not to worry ladies and gentlemen," Enzo told the novatus that surrounded him. "All this means is that we'll be starting our next round of human cleansing *early!*"

With a snap of his fingers, the sixty or so half-drunken and previously celebrating novatus bounded into battle upon Enzo's request. With a point of his fingers, Franz Kaymore ordered his hundreds of golden knights to do the same. The two groups clashed together over a battlefield of rubble and stone, with weapons clanging and elements flying.

While Enzo charged alongside his army into battle, Kaymore hung back with the section of his men who used the cannon to take down novatus from a distance. The novatus cannon fodder victims worked to dwindle their numbers, heavily increasing the human's already imposing numbers advantage by a considerable margin. But the novatus still fought bravely, especially with Kane at the front lines, his fists burning with surging balls of flames as he beat golden knights to a pulp.

***

Back at the peninsula, the Novatus Protection Centre seemed to finally be recovering from the immense effects of Reyan's attack weeks prior. Through the combined efforts of the surviving Kin of Land and Kin of Man higher-ups, they managed to rebuild again. To add to the relatively good news, Protector Bianca was back in action. Besides the scars that dragged down from her face to her body and a hobble in her walk, she had made a complete recovery.

Protector Bianca slowly walked through the halls of the main building. They were vastly emptier and less trainee-filled than she was used to seeing them. Protector Bianca frowned at the sight. She had noticed fewer novatus trainees around since Reyan's massacre. The absence of the novatus she spent the most time with bothered her the most. She recalled seeing Dillon Fachmann fall in that very battle and although she remembered Gabriel Elijah and Magnolia Thorne surviving the battle, she had seen no sight of them ever since she woke up. To add to that, she had not seen Kane Keahi return either. The Protector could only wonder what had happened whilst she was comatose.

Bianca made her way to a stone-doored room guarded by two men, one of which was sleeping on the job. With a flick of her ice-covered fingers, Bianca used her abilities to wake up the man and knock both out of the way.

"Thank you for your service, boys," Protector Bianca told them sarcastically.

"No problem, Protector," one of them groaned.

Bianca entered the stone inventory and immediately saw to sorting out and sifting through all of the scrolls. As she sorted out and filed the scrolls, she noticed a pattern - over a dozen scrolls were missing by her count as well as three maps. This bothered her to no end.

She marched over to the end of the room and looked for one scroll in particular. She arrived there to see the scroll dictating information on The Brew of Tranquillity was missing.

"Oh no…" she sighed.

***

The war between Kaymore and Caelestis' armies raged on in the most destructive manner possible. Most of the castle had broken down with the battlefield having stretched out past the debris of the halls and dining palace, with a good portion of the fighting taking place on the further fields.

Thus far, the fight was not looking up in Enzo's army's favour. Whilst his bolts of lightning and blades of air took down knight after knight, the rest of his clan struggled against the humans and their superior numbers. A large section of the novatus front fell victim to Kaymore's cannon. Firing at them relentlessly.

As the battle continued, the half-drunk Selene struggled to maintain control over her powers once again. Intensely focused, she barely managed to successfully take down the knights with her dark water waves.

Magnolia fought with all her might, vines ejecting out of her and blocking gold swords as the enemies attacked. Dodging a flurry of attacks, she realised she needed a better defence. With haste, she built a tall tree of vines, wrapping herself up to a higher vantage point to fight from.

Kane fought recklessly using heat and passion to maim his enemies with gruesome and specific attacks. His slicing flames burned the arm of a knight so brutally it crumbled itself off of his body. As the man cried tears of pure agony, Kane collected the crisped remains of his fallen arm and force-fed them into his wailing mouth.

While he force-fed the gold knight, a series of knights rushed at the opportunity to attack him whilst distracted. Just as Kane was to be cut to pieces, Gabriel flew past the knights and picked Kane up. He whisked Kane away from danger, as the two landed on a field a few metres away from the battle. Kane leapt back up to his feet, equally annoyed and grateful for Gabriel's intervention.

"You're welcome," Gabriel snarked at him.

"Yes, yes, you're my hero," Kane grunted back sarcastically. He generated fire out of the palm of both hands and flew his way back into the thick of battle.

Gabriel scoffed. He shook his head and flew in the opposite direction to Kane, coming to the aid of Selene and Magnolia in battle.

Selene was slowly but surely sobering up, with her body starting to meet an equilibrium as she moved with the waves of water she controlled. Magnolia had also started to find her footing in the battle, knocking knights back with a set of sturdy vine attacks. Gabriel joined, doing his part to aid with waves of air attacks.

Enzo decapitated a knight-guard with a sword of lightning, the blue sizzling shock contrasting against the red flurry of spurting blood. He surveyed the vast battlefield to see how well the clan was starting to fair as a whole. The most wicked of smiles developed as he basked in the destruction that surrounded him. The novatus had started to truly take control of this battle.

Within a matter of seconds, this marvellous sight that Enzo had just admired was instantly destroyed.

Hundreds of cannonballs suddenly took flight from all different directions, a series of deceptively quick iron ammunition peppering them as fast as the eye could see. Members of the novatus clan were unable to use their elemental powers to dodge and avoid the cannons in time. Some were frozen in fear, while others were caught off-guard completely, leaving the cannonballs to knock them down and blast them to pieces. In under a minute, the battle advantage the novatus clan harboured had waned significantly.

Enzo growled in frustration, his eyes darting around to see where the cannons were coming from. With the smoke he saw rising in the distance, all became clear. Kaymore had called in reinforcements. He watched a further cavalry of gold knights swarm, two extra armies from both sides of the battlefield. The ground quaked as the gold knights charged towards them, their swords drawn and ready for battle.

Enzo screamed with anger as the reinforcements of gold knights dominated his novatus army. Kaymore laughed, watching his men besiege and destroy with glee.

With a panicked leap, Enzo bounded into the air and flew amongst the clouds. From high above he harvested electricity with his hands, forming it into continuous bolts of lightning. He rained these bolts of energy down on the gold knights in a desperate attempt to salvage the battle.

But it was of no use. More of his army was being decimated faster than his lightning, and Kaymore's army was advancing.

The skies darkened grey as Enzo let out a frustrated yelp, desperately summoning lightning from the heavens. The display of power crackled in the air, illuminating the battlefield with its bright light. As Enzo prepared to unleash his attack, he was shot out of commission with Kaymore's cannon. Three fastballs made their way from the muzzle of the cannon to Enzo's midsection in the blink of an eye, blasting him out of the air.

He fell from the sky, his once-grand vision of the battlefield was reduced to a hellish wasteland. He watched in horror as the gold-knight armies systematically mowed down the remaining novatus.

Cannonballs continued to rain down from the sky, sending warriors flying and blasting them to pieces. Enzo tried to stand, but the pain was too much to bear. He fell to the floor where he writhed in excruciating pain. Blood dripped from his mouth onto the ground as he was forced to witness the novatus he had led into battle fall one by one.

Gabriel, Magnolia, and Selene were amongst the survivors, huddled together as they made a last-ditch effort to fight back. Gabriel flew into the air, unleashing wind strikes on the incoming knights, but they were too many to deal with. Both girls had too little energy to sufficiently aid in his attacks, with Selene unable to even lift her arms due to aching.

Magnolia formed another tree of sturdy vines around them, protecting them from the onslaught of knights ready to strike at their weakness. Choosing flight over fight, Magnolia desperately encapsulated the three of them in a tree of vines. Using the full extent of her flora abilities, she stretched them far away from the battlefield with a jolting set of vines.

With the trio having retreated, the remaining novatus followed them in fleeing the battlegrounds. Only a few of them managed to escape, with most being chased and cut down by Kaymore's armies. Soon, there were only a handful of clan members speckled across the vast battlefield.

With Enzo laying helpless on the ground, Franz Kaymore was carried towards him by his knights. Franz leered over the writhing Enzo; his face twisted with malicious intent. He seized a sword off of one of his guards and raised it above Enzo. He was more than ready to deliver the killing blow and put the battle to bed. Yet he would not get to.

A blinding light burst in front of him and his legion. An illumination so intense that it blocked their vision, causing them to stagger back. As the light dissipated, Franz and his knights saw one final novatus who remained standing: Kane, with both arms encased in fire.

Kane stood in front of Franz and his legion, sweating, panting, and holding a violent look in his eyes. He was all that stood between them and killing Enzo.

BATTLE AT THE CASTLE OF DEBRIS II

Kane stood his ground, blocking Kaymore and his army from reaching Enzo.

The Caelestis clan leader slowly stood himself back on his feet. "Thank you," he coughed as he shook off the pain. He surveyed the area once more to see Kaymore's men continuing to grow in numbers, with legions rushing towards them from across the battlefield.

"Get out of the way before I drive this sword through you too!" Kaymore commanded.

Kane laughed in the face of the Grand Leader and his hundreds of knights. "I'd rather die than take orders from a pathetic human," he asserted. "Especially one as fat, ugly, and useless as *you*."

Kaymore's face flushed red with anger. With the point of his sword, he ordered his knights to execute them both. The legions of gold knights surrounded Kane and Enzo, their weapons drawn and ready to strike.

Kane enhanced the intensity of the fire that encased both his arms, flames flicking up to his elbows. Enzo harnessed wind in his palms and crackling lightning around his fists. The pair stood back-to-back as hundreds of gold knights closed in.

Together, they unleashed their elemental powers to the fullest extent as the gold knights charged at them, swords raised high. They moved with blinding speed, dodging, and striking with deadly precision. Fire and lightning clashed with steel and armour, illuminating the battlefield with bursts of passionate light.

As they fought, Franz Kaymore bellowed orders to his men, urging them to cut down the novatus with all their might. But Kane and Enzo were too skilled for them. They weaved in and out of the knights' attacks, creating openings for themselves with bursts of flame and gusts of wind. The gold knights fell one by one, their armour melted by the intense heat and their bodies electrified by the shocking lightning.

Franz grew more enraged as he watched his army being dealt with by just two novatus. He ordered his cannons to fire at Kane and Enzo, hoping to take them out with a single blast. But Kane and Enzo were too quick for them. They dodged the cannonballs with ease, using their powers of wind and fire to propel themselves out of harm's way.

Kane rushed towards the right side of the battlefield, drawing half of the knights with him. Enzo followed suit, running towards the left side of the battlefield, and drawing the other half of the knights with him. The gold knights charged after them, determined to cut them down.

Kane covered his territory with the wildest of fires, flames licking at the knights' armour and melting it away. Enzo generated whirling winds around his area, whipping up tornadoes that tossed the gold knights like rag dolls. The two novatus took the army head-on, with nothing but raw vigour to pull them through.

***

The battle raged on for what seemed like hours, with no end in sight. The gold knights fell one by one, their bodies broken and burned. Though for every knight that fell, two more took their place. Kane and Enzo were starting to tire, their powers waning as they fought on. Yet they continued to fight, refusing to let up.

More gold knights swarmed the pair, their weapons glinting in the sunlight. Kaymore shouted orders at them, urging them to cut and fire cannons at the two novatus fighters. The deep pockets of the Kaymore Family war front showed to be even deeper with dozens of reinforcements rushing into battle on horseback. The swords and cannons the two novatus had been evading with ease were rapidly increasing in numbers and becoming harder to handle.

As the battle wore on, Kane and Enzo started to lose their grip on the fight. Their movements became slower and less precise as they grew tired and battered. They fled from the thick of it and regrouped in the centre of the battlefield, back-to-back once again.

With each passing second, their fighting became sloppier, whereas the gold knights only felt more encouraged to swarm and kill. Kaymore's army pressed further and further, insistent on applying pressure to the two novatus. As time went on, it was clear to see that no amount of raw skill from the clan leader and the Kin of Sun would be able to keep up with the number of soldiers compounding on them at once. With each punch, kick, and elemental blast, their bodies tired, energy depleting. Kaymore's knights were eager to capitalise on this.

A knight landed a crippling blow on Enzo, impaling him through the leg with his golden sword. Enzo stumbled over, losing his footing in battle. Fear flickered in his eyes as he saw himself immediately ambushed by dozens of knights, ready to pounce on his sudden weakness.

His body was cut and slashed with multiple guards revelling at the prospect of finally being able to strike him. Kane was too busy dealing with his half of the army to aid him, allowing dozens more knights to jump at the opportunity to cut him down.

Enzo screamed in visceral agony, his body in deep pain and his mind fractured and racing. The spectre of death lurked, yet he refused to allow himself to be taken by its grasp. Amid desperation, an unsavoury idea ignited.

Enzo charged lightning from the base of his arm to the tip of his finger. He extended it outwards in a blistering attack. Not towards any of the knights, but towards Kane.

Kane was brought to his knees, shocked both physically and mentally as Enzo's attack struck him down. Gold knights wasted no time, pouncing on him with exacerbating attacks.

With more fighters rushing toward Kane, Enzo took the opportunity to escape. He leapt to the sky via a gust of wind and flew away, leaving Kane to face the fighting alone.

"Enzo?!" Kane called as he saw the clan leader fly. He dodged blows from surrounding gold knights as he waited to see if Enzo would be coming back.

He did not. The leader of the Clan of Caelestis flew over the horizon, well and truly leaving Kane to deal with the swarms on his own.

"CURSE YOU CAELESTIS!" he screamed at the top of his lungs.

Regardless of the circumstances, Kane refused to give in. He continued the battle on his own, but with each swing of his arms, it became clear that he was too tired and weak to fight them all. He retreated, using his fire generation to escape from the crowd.

Due to how feeble his powers had become from constant usage; he could only soar for a few metres before crashing to the ground. The fierce and ferocious novatus found himself desperate and panting as the army of gold knights closed in on him once again. They surged with purpose, many scores strong, gearing up to put him to the sword.

Kane closed his eyes and braced himself for the inevitable as the knights drew closer and closer, inches away from execution. He took a deep breath and waited for the killing blow. He tensed himself, accepting his fate.

Suddenly, he felt a vine wrap around his leg and yank him away, forceful, and swift.

He opened his eyes in surprise to see himself moving at insane speeds as the vine pulled him through the air. Too weak to do otherwise, Kane let the animated plant take him wherever it may.

The vine eventually snapped, and he tumbled on the floor for the dozenth time that day. The Kin of Sun grunted in pain and rolled over, struggling to catch his breath. Turning over onto his backside, saw that the vine had pulled him onto a faraway field of roses. He gazed into the distance, seeing the legions of Kaymore's knights still charging through the fields around the fallen castle. Kane was miles away from a killing blow now.

He pivoted to see Gabriel, Selene, and Magnolia were all behind him, the wind flowing through the roses at their feet. Selene lay on the floor, panting heavily, while Magnolia moved her hands. She used her abilities to retract the vine that pulled Kane to safety, from a vine tree that was sprouting out of the ground behind her.

Kane stared at the trio in silence, a dejected look about him who all looked back at him with sympathy. Kane avoided their gazes. He glared down at nothing in particular, his fists clenching at the roses beneath him.

Gabriel crouched down and offered a hand out to Kane. Kane gritted his teeth, seeming as if he was going to reject it. With reluctance, he accepted Gabriel's hand. Gabriel pulled Kane onto his feet, Kane steadying himself upwards.

As the calming winds beat their faces, the novatus rivals stared at each other with silent tension. Neither of them had uttered a word, yet the looks in their eyes spoke a thousand.

Gabriel placed a soft hand on Kane's shoulder. "Let's leave this land," he said, breaking the silence.

"Yeah," Kane agreed with a sigh. "Let's."

NOW ENTERING RECKONEN ASYLUM

"Are you officially part of our gang now Kang?" Selene asked as the quartet marched their way through a dingy cobbled side street behind a series of homes with mould on the outside walls.

"Kane," he corrected. "And I've known the people in your 'gang' longer than you have."

"You know what I meant. Are you really up for making The Brew of Tranquillity with us?" asked Selene. "Like are you really seriously actually up for it?"

"Yes," sighed Kane. "I am."

"Good. It's nice having you here with us," Magnolia beamed. Kane kissed his teeth at her, subtly irritated.

"He's only with us because that Enzo guy betrayed him though." Selene chuckled.

Gabriel and Magnolia shot her warning glares, a non-verbal order to cease talking.

"What? It happened days ago! Thought it would be fine to joke about it by now," Selene defended herself. "Is it not?"

Gabriel and Magnolia shook their heads at her. Kane paid no mind to Selene's remarks, staring straight ahead as if he had not heard her.

The four of them walked near the end of the side street, towards a bend that would lead them out to the neighbourhood proper.

Kane's face twisted, unimpressed by his surroundings. "How long until we reach our destination?" he asked. Gabriel slung his sack bag off of his shoulder and picked a scrolled-up map out of it.

"It should be somewhere around here, shouldn't it?" Kane added.

"You're right, it should be close by," Gabriel said as he looked over the map.

The four walked for a few more minutes until they reached the end of the alleyway. They walked around the bend and out into a long and wide-open street of jagged rock.

Across from the outstretching street, a half mile away, was a dark maroon obelisk block of a building several stories, hundreds of feet tall with gates all around it and guards outside of it.

"There it is," said Gabriel as the four of them looked upon the staggering entrance of Reckonen Asylum.

The quartet carefully observed the Asylum building, gates and those who guarded them. They looked less like the usual knights or soldiers that would guard enclosures such as this, and more like thugs pulled off of the streets. Instead of clean-cut men in uniforms or armour, the guards were brash muscular men dressed in tattered plain robes and tunics. Instead of swords, lances and maces, the scabbard belts around their waists held bloody knives and long whips.

"Why are we here again?" asked Selene with a raised eyebrow.

"I was kind of wondering the same," Magnolia snarked.

"When I was looking for Kane in Kicen Village, Layla listed here as one of the only places where you'll find a large congregation of novatus. We should be able to find a Kin of Beasts and Kin of Man to join us for the Brew here," explained Gabriel. "It's also not too far from the Prisoner's Forest."

"Getting into Reckonen Asylum is bad enough. I wouldn't advise trying to get into the Prisoners Forest too," warned Kane.

"Right," said Gabriel with a nodded head. "Let's hope we can find what we need here alone."

"So, are we going to try and get in then?" asked Selene.

"Once we figure out a way to get in safely," said Gabriel.

The four hid behind the wall at the end of the side street, carefully watching over the Asylum's entrance. They looked around the area, waiting for any clue as to how they could get in. After twenty minutes of waiting, something finally happened.

A very tall man toting a large wheelbarrow walked his way over from another street and towards the Asylum entrance. The quartet looked in closer to see what was being carried in his wheelbarrow. In it, one dozen injured and sick young novatus lay piled up on top of one another as an elemental essence buzzed around them.

The man was permitted to enter the premises, the guards parting ways and opening the gates for him. He wheeled the barrow of ill novatus past the gates and up to the dark crimson entrance door to the building where he stopped in his tracks. He waited patiently by the door for a few minutes, until it opened.

A young woman exited the building. She was of slim body, average height, and carried a shaky presence about her. She sported long brown hair and two thin circular crystals fixed over both of her eyes.

"Your morning shipment, Ms George," the man grunted to her as he gestured down.

She smiled as she greeted the wheelbarrow man with a firm handshake. Once they were done shaking hands, the man left the wheelbarrow to her and walked away, leaving the premises.

Ms George inspected the pile of sick novatus with quiet buzzing excitement about her. She spent a while simply marvelling at all the novatus that were delivered to her, running her finger along each of their skulls with a beaming smile on her face.

Kane narrowed his eyes as he watched her wheel the novatus into the building, the door shutting firmly behind her. "I know how we can get in," he told the other three.

***

The guards surrounding the gates of Reckonen Asylum remained vigilant as they scanned the area for potential threats to the Asylum. As far as they were concerned, no person—human, novatus, or otherwise—was anywhere near enough to the general vicinity to cause any problems. No activity whatsoever.

The echoing sounds of a giant explosion rattled the asylum guards, pulling them out of their peaceful observance. Their attention was immediately forced towards one of the neighbourhoods in the distance. Behind these mouldy-walled houses, a cloud of smoke, fire, and dark energy formed. A great portion of the guards left their station, twenty men rushing to the scene of the explosion.

These guards returned several minutes later with their hands full. Within the hands of four of these guards were Gabriel, Magnolia, Selene, and Kane, barely conscious, shivering, and covered in soot and ash. The guards took the four of them past the gates and to the main entrance where one of them knocked on the door so hard it shook. The men waited for moments on end before the door opened and Ms George finally returned. Without as much as another word, Ms George's eyes darted towards the four dirtied and barely conscious novatus that were brought to her doorstep.

"Brilliant!" she chuffed as she urged the men to bring them in. Gabriel, Selene, Magnolia, and Kane pretended to be too injured and ill to move or even open their eyes as they were carried.

As the four were brought further into the asylum, Kane opened his eyes slightly to get a better look at their surroundings as they were transported. Kane saw the layout of the Asylum was very similar to all of the novatus shelters he had been in, though with some slight differences. Instead of healthy novatus being ushered around by Protectors, he saw battered and bruised novatus being ushered around by the guards. Instead of somewhat cosy dorms constructed of wood and leaves, they were dull staying rooms made of maroon stone. And instead of novatus wandering the halls and letting their abilities fly under careful supervision, novatus wandered the halls with their heads downwards and walked through the area frightened, under strict supervision. A series of sights that disgusted Kane to no end.

The four were taken into a private room. They were placed on a wide table in a medical centre cluttered with shelves of potions and fixed on every wall. The guards left them there, alone in the room with Ms George.

"Wonderful creatures," she whispered as she inspected each of their bodies. She ran her fingers across the three of them carefully one at a time, until she reached Kane.

"Especially you," she whispered to him. "You're going to be one of my favourites."

Ms George slowly reached underneath Kane's trousers, her hands making their way up his leg.

Kane decided she had gone far enough, opening his eyes, and revealing that he was fully conscious the whole time. In a matter of seconds, he was on his feet and threatening her with a fist full of fire only centimetres away from her face. Selene, Gabriel, and Magnolia followed suit, jumping off the table and blocking her path. Ms George was surrounded and backed into a corner. Though instead of being frightened, anxious or feeling the urge to scream for her guards as the group might have anticipated, she remained unbothered.

She stared back at them with a nonchalant look on her face. "Very wonderful creatures," she laughed quietly.

"How 'wonderful' would it be if I were to burn the skin off of your face right now?" Kane threatened.

"I don't see why you'd do that," she said flippantly.

"You don't see why a group of novatus would want to fight back against being trapped in a room so you can study and defile them?" scoffed Kane.

"Who said you were trapped here?" she asked genuinely.

Kane furrowed his brows at her, the other three novatus shared his confusion.

"You don't expect us to believe for we can just leave when your guards locked us in here?" Gabriel asked. "This is a novatus asylum, after all."

"Yes, *Reckonen* Asylum. Not Reckonen *Prison*," Ms George giggled, casually walking away from Kane and his fire-fist.

She moved past the other three and went to the door which she unlocked with a key. "You don't have to stay in here if you don't want to," she told them.

Kane lowered his fist, extinguishing the fire around it. He joined the others who stared at Ms George by the open door, still harbouring confused faces.

"So, we're free to go anywhere we want?" asked Magnolia.

"Anywhere in the *Asylum*," Ms George answered with emphasis.

"For real?" asked Selene.

"Of course," said Ms George in a low yet soft voice. "How am I meant to study your behaviour if you're locked up?"

Alessandra flashed a great big smile at the four, its brightness matching the crystals that covered her eyes.

"Right," Kane said, wary.

With care and caution, the quartet made their way out of the room. As they walked out, Kane felt he could still feel Alessandra's smiling gaze, as if it was burning through the back of his head.

***

The quartet made their way through one of the halls that lead to a series of staying rooms for the other asylum captives. As they huddled together, they saw four guards watching them from down the other end of the hall. Unfortunately, this seemed to be the closest they would get to privacy for the time being.

"Alright, so what's the plan?" asked Magnolia during their conversation of whispers.

"Well since we know we can roam around here freely; I say we split up and look for powerful novatus of the two classes we don't have yet," suggested Gabriel.

"We just need Kin of Man and Beasts, right?" asked Selene.

"Right,"

"I think we should focus on finding a Kin of Beasts, they're the rarest class," suggested Kane. Gabriel nodded in agreement with him.

"But what do we even do if we find 'em? Just blurt out the Brew of Tranquillity story and hope they're inspired to join?" asked Selene.

"Not much else we can do really," sighed Magnolia.

"Then let's split up and get to it," asserted Gabriel. "I don't think we'll find anyone too powerful on the first few floors. Kane, you look through the north side of the fifth floor whilst Magnolia takes the south. I'll look at the north side of the sixth floor and Selene at the south. We'll meet back here two and a half hours from now at the latest. Okay?"

All three nodded in agreement with Gabriel. The quartet left the safety of their huddles of whispers and embarked up the stairs and across the different regions of the asylum to carry out their plans.

✳✳✳

Selene skipped through the halls of the south side of the sixth floor. She whistled cheerfully as she bounded past all of the staying rooms that filled that side of the floor. Her optimistic attitude as she skipped around heavily contrasted against all of the other novatus whom she passed by on her search. She stuck out like a sore thumb to the point where some of the guards started to take notice of her.

***

As Kane made his way through the north side of the fifth floor, he found a more open space of novatus than Selene. He happened upon what looked like a prisoners' mess hall with novatus being served food on trays from a run-down canteen to take and eat at their cinder block tables. Though the area was hardly used for its intended purpose. Kane had only been watching the asylum members get their food for a minute before a fight broke out. Two women, a Kin of Skies and a Kin of Land had accidentally bumped into one another and within the blink of an eye, they were throwing food and elements at each other as the other asylum members egged them on with screams. The fight only stopped when a dozen guards showed up at the scene with heavy whips dozens of feet long. The guards whipped the woman until they stopped fighting, then whipped all the people who had egged on their fight. Kane shook his head in disappointment.

***

Almost an hour into his search around the north side of the sixth floor, Gabriel was yet to find a single person suitable to help with The Brew of Tranquillity as he looked through all of the windows of the staying rooms. Of all the people Gabriel saw both through these rooms and passing by him in the halls, the strongest candidates were a young Kin of Beasts who could only transform into a small owl and an elderly Kin of Man with only one leg.

He stopped in the middle of one of the hallways, a bright shining light capturing his attention. He looked upwards to see the light was being generated from a purple crystal on the roof of the very top of the building. The crystal acted as a painted window allowing the sun to pass through it and amplify the light. He noticed that this large crystal window plain resembled the same crystals that Ms George used to cover both her eyes. Though he did not see her around anywhere, Gabriel could not shake the intense feeling that he was still being watched by her and her creepy smile.

***

Magnolia was having a similar experience to Gabriel, not finding anyone as she made her way through the halls of the fifth floor's south side. She walked past staying room after staying room, hall after hall, seeing nothing but weak, ill, and bandaged novatus. Almost an hour and a half into her search and Magnolia was all but ready to give up and return to their meeting point early. Until she saw something promising at the very end of a hall she embarked on.

Magnolia saw a glimpse of the inside of a large staying room. Unlike the other rooms around the area, there were only a handful of guards around. This hall was also booming with the noises of a room full of novatus who not only sounded as if they wanted to be there, they were celebrating. She hurried her way down the hall and towards the staying room of loud celebrations.

Magnolia entered through the open door to see crowds of asylum members had gathered for a party. The room had been constructed into a makeshift bar with men serving stone mugs of alcohol off of cinder block bar counters from each corner. She sifted her way through the crowds of drunk and partying novatus who occupied the spacious staying room. She made her way towards the very end of the room where another crowd was gathering around a mid-sized cinder block stage. She smiled in confusion as she looked at the cheering novatus around her who clapped their hands as they looked onto the stage.

"What's going on here?" Magnolia asked a young man next to her in the crowd.

"That cool Kin of Man guy is going to perform again!" said the man excitedly, drunkenly slurring his words a little. "These are the only good parts of my week. I can't fucking wait!"

"Who's the cool Kin of Man guy?" Magnolia asked with bewilderment. The drunken man ignored her and looked back to the small cinder block stage. She shrugged and looked to where he was looking.

Parting through the crowds that surrounded the stage came a large young man. He was a towering six feet three inches tall, with a toned slender frame. He pushed his way past all of the people that gathered and climbed on top of the cinder block. The crowd went wild as soon as they saw him plant his feet on the stage. Magnolia looked the man up and down as he basked in the attention that was bestowed upon him. He had a thick head of dirty blonde hair, soft greyish-blue eyes, and a cheekily charming demeanour about him. Like the rest of the crowd, she could not take her eyes off him.

Asylum members threw a set of knives and swords at the 'cool Kin of Man guy.' He expertly caught two swords and one knife in each of his hands without a hassle. The crowd cheered him on as he started to juggle all of the knives and swords, throwing them into the air and catching them again at insane speeds. With every blade he threw in the air and caught back again, it looked as if he could never fail. The more the crowd cheered him on, the quicker juggled the blades. He threw each blade even higher into the air as he juggled it. The crowd watched in awesome glory as the man succeeded in not dropping the blades or even cutting himself once. The Kin of Man saw how excited the crowd was becoming and decided to increase the speed and throwing heights at which he juggled. This was not his best idea.

Though he succeeded in throwing and catching five of the six blades, the speed at which he was throwing and catching meant he miscalculated the last one. The last knives came soaring down towards the man at too quick of a speed for him to dodge. The blade struck him across the face, leaving a huge open wound down his cheek and onto his neck. The crowd went silent with shock as the man dropped to the floor with a deep gash on his face...

...but then, the man used his advanced Kin of Man abilities to accelerate his healing factor. Within seconds the wound closed up, and the man leapt back up on his feet. He stretched his arms out as the crowd went wild for him once again. They laughed and cried as the cool Kin of Man rubbed the part of his face where the wound had healed. With a proud bow, he ended the show. The asylum members gave him a rousing round of applause, delighted by what they had just witnessed. Including Magnolia.

***

Later, much after his 'show' had concluded, the cool Kin of Man guy sat on a cinder block on his own in the corner of the room. He had filled the largest stone mug he could find with alcohol, guzzling it down on his lonesome as the crowd that once adored him had their attention focused elsewhere. One person, however, still had their eyes set on him. He was more than happy to see them come his way.

"Hello," he greeted Magnolia as she nervously approached him. With a smile on his face, he stood up from his block and fixed his hair

159

with a swipe of a hand through it. "Don't think I've seen you here before. What's your name?"

"Magnolia." She introduced herself, twirling her fine white hair in her finger as she looked up at him.

"Magnolia? What a weird yet wonderfully beautiful name." he flirted.

Magnolia rolled her eyes at him, her cheeks blushing red. "And what's your name?" she asked.

"Henry," he answered. "Henry Adam."

"Very nice to meet you, Henry Adam," Magnolia said as she offered her hand. Henry accepted Magnolia's handshake delicately. The two novatus longingly stared into each other's eyes as they shook hands.

LUST AND PERSUASION

The whereabouts of Nathanael Reyan were often a mystery to most people of the all kingdoms. With his grand fleet of ships that seemed to move at sonic speed through the seas he could travel to any of the Four Kingdoms within no more than a day or two, meaning if he and his Vyre soldiers were not protecting the land or hunting novatus, he could be anywhere.

Reyan spent his time bathing in a river below a mountain, that day. He spent his time there, on his lonesome, the rest of his fleet and soldiers nowhere to be seen. As he bathed, a strange occurrence took place. The longer he spent in the water, the more his skin hardened and glowed.

***

Magnolia and Henry sat on the cinder blocks. They drank as they leaned on the walls of the party-crazed staying room, deep in conversation with one another.

"So, you do this every week?" Magnolia asked.

"Yep. Every Tuesday and Friday, they come down here to watch me do that exact performance," answered Henry.

"They all come to watch you do the same thing twice a week?" she asked incredulously.

"Yeah!" Henry laughed. "Apparently it never gets old. Shows how bored we all are here."

Magnolia giggled, shaking her head.

Henry took another guzzle of alcohol from his stone mug, then sighed with laughter. "Like I said, I've not seen you here before." he repeated. "When were you taken in?"

"Today," Magnolia answered.

"Just today? No wonder I've not seen you here before."

"Yeah, I've only been around the Asylum for a few hours now," said Magnolia. "What about you? Seems like you've been here for ages."

"Nah, just a few months," answered Henry.

"Oh right, cool," said Magnolia, nodding her head. "So how is it here?"

Henry paused in the middle of another swig from the mug. He had no drink in his mouth, yet his throat gulped as if to force something down.

"It's good staying here I guess," he said with a smile on his face yet hesitancy in his voice. "Really good."

"Are you ever allowed to leave though?" asked Magnolia. Henry shook his head with reluctance as if he did not want to give her that answer. She noticed the mountains of confidence he had previously seeping out of him via his body language.

"But why would any of us want to? We get to sleep and eat here for free, safe from all the hassle of the rest of the Kingdom." he rationalised. "We also get to roam around the asylum and do whatever we want… as long as we allow Ms George to perform a few 'routine tests on us."

"Routine tests?" Magnolia asked with concern.

"It's nothing major," Henry tried to assure her. "Just Alessandra and a couple of her guard's kind of prodding you, measuring you and taking notes on how you react to certain potions on your skin whilst you sleep. You barely notice it, it's nothing to worry about."

"It kind of sounds like something to worry about!" exclaimed Magnolia. "How the hell are you okay with people messing with you whilst you're trying to sleep!"

Henry chuckled. In an instance, Magnolia watched as that confident energy returned. "If you're really worried about it, I'll make sure to keep an eye on you since we're sleeping together tonight," he said with a smirk.

"Excuse me?" gasped Magnolia. "What exactly do you mean by that?"

"This room here is one large set of connected staying rooms that me and a bunch of guys and girls share. If you get assigned to one of the side rooms then you'll technically be sleeping together with a whole bunch of us," he explained nonchalantly. "Why, what did you think I meant?"

Magnolia narrowed her eyes at Henry. Henry attempted to keep a straight face but he could not for the life of him. He placed his stone mug in front of his mouth to hide his giggling. His laughter proved contagious; Magnolia no longer capable of holding her scowl.

"I can already tell. You're a cheeky one, aren't you?" she commented with a smirk on her face.

"Maybe I am," Henry laughed with a shrug. "But you like that don't you?"

Magnolia smiled back at Henry. Once again, the two lost themselves in each other's eyes.

***

Much later, Kane turned around the corner and entered one of the halls on the first floor. There he found Gabriel and Selene waiting impatiently at the agreed-upon meeting spot.

"Found anyone eligible yet?" Kane asked as he joined them in another huddle of whispers.

"Not yet," answered Gabriel. Selene shook her head.

"Great," Kane scoffed sarcastically.

"Also, have either of you seen Magnolia?" Gabriel asked.

"Nope," Selene answered. Kane shook his head.

Gabriel huffed out a sigh of vexation. "It's well past the agreed meeting time," he complained. "Where could she be?"

Whilst the three of them waited on her, Magnolia spent her time with Henry in one of the sleeping rooms within the large staying room he told her about. The pair lay on a plush mattress, passionately kissing as they dry-humped each other. The two novatus looked just about ready to take off each other's clothes and begin the motions of love-making. Henry had already taken off his tunic shirt and was about to help Magnolia take off hers.

But before he could, Magnolia got cold feet. All of a sudden, she stopped kissing him, springing up from on top of him and leaving the mattress to stand in the corner.

"Is something wrong?" Henry asked as he sat up on the mattress.

"My Lord, how could I let myself get carried away like that?!" Magnolia gasped, cleaning up her hair and clothes as she paced back and forth.

"Did you not want to get with me?" Henry asked, confused.

"I did but…that's not what I was planning to do when I introduced myself to you," explained Magnolia.

Henry's face was as blank and confused as one could ever be. "What *were* you planning to do then?" he asked.

Magnolia made strict eye contact with Henry once more. Though as she stared at him this time, it was not with a look of lust but a look of concern. She rolled her tongue within the inside of her mouth with reluctance, until she finally said:

"Have you heard of the story of The Brew of Tranquillity?"

Henry sighed. "Can't say I have, no."

Magnolia nodded, slowly walking back to him, and sitting down on the mattress. "Then let me tell you."

***

Gabriel, Selene, and Kane remained within the halls of the first floor of the Asylum, impatiently awaiting Magnolia's arrival.

"Ugh, she's taking forever," Selene groaned as she slid across the wall.

165

A couple of guards who had been keeping their eye on the trio approached from across the hall.

"Is everything alright young ones?" asked one of the thuggish guards as the two of them stood in front of them. Selene ignored them, Gabriel gazed at them with apprehension and Kane directly glared at them. He cast a quick look at one of their hands where a large long whip hung.

"We're fine," Kane responded with venom.

"Well if you're having any problems, let us know," said the other guard.

"Alright," Gabriel responded, giving a nod. The guards nodded back and left for their original stations. With them far enough away again, the trio returned to their huddle.

"I don't like how those guards are starting to hover around us," Kane said.

"I know, we must look suspicious standing around here for so long," said Gabriel.

"Let's go exploring around the Asylum then," Selene suggested excitedly.

"Let's go to where Magnolia was searching," Gabriel offered as an alternative to Selene's idea. "Hopefully we'll find her again."

The three of them made their way away from the hallway and towards the nearest staircase.

***

"...we need you to fill the role of Kin of Man. So that we can make progress towards creating The Brew of Tranquillity," Magnolia said, finishing a lengthy explanation.

Henry held the same blank and confused look on his face that he had when she first brought up the concept. She sat there for a short while, waiting for him to say anything in response. Instead of speaking, Henry snickered.

"What part of anything I just told you was funny?" Magnolia asked in annoyance.

"The part where I thought I was going to spend the afternoon sleeping with a gorgeous girl but instead she just wants to talk me into her and her friends' far-fetched plan to 'save our people'," Henry laughed.

"It's not far-fetched and we *are* going to save our people!" she insisted.

"Yeah right," laughed Henry.

Magnolia sighed. Now she knew how Gabriel felt when he tried to convince Kane.

"It was a very entertaining story and I'd love to be of help to you and your friends but…it doesn't exactly appeal to me,"

"What part of saving your people doesn't appeal to you?"

"The part where I have to run around across the Kingdoms risking death."

"So what? Would you rather just rot away *here* for the rest of your life?"

Henry paused for a moment to think. "Well, not exactly," he sighed. "But I still don't want-"

Magnolia seized Henry by the arm and dragged him out of the sleeping room. In an angered huff she pulled him through the main staying room, pushing past all of the people who were crowded around the area.

"Where are you taking me?!" Henry asked querulously. He tried to yank himself out of Magnolia's grasp only for her to generate a series of vines that tied her hand to his. He was unable to pull himself away from her, forced to go along with wherever she was taking him.

Magnolia retracted the vines once the two of them had reached the nearest window within the halls of the sixth floor - a hole in the stone walls of the building with so many bars blocking it a fly would struggle to escape.

"Look out there," Magnolia ordered.

"Why? What for?" he questioned as he peered out of the window. All he could see from this vantage point were distant glimpses of long grass fields and empty neighbourhoods.

"When was the last time you stepped even a foot out there?" Magnolia asked.

"This morning," Henry lied.

Magnolia raised an eyebrow at him and crossed her arms.

"Not once since I was taken here," he admitted with a sigh.

"Exactly. And something tells me that if you did try and go out there, *Ms Alessandra George* would put a swift end to it. Right?" she said.

Henry took a deep dejected breath. He turned to the side, avoiding answering her question. Magnolia closed the distance between the two of them and rested a hand on his shoulder.

"But if you join us, Henry, we'll not just get you out of here. We'll make The Brew and bring in a world where novatus can go wherever they want in whatever Kingdom they choose," she promised. Henry lowered his eyes. He raised his head back up again to look at her.

"Magnolia?" called out a deep male voice, interrupting their moment.

Magnolia and Henry shifted around to see Gabriel, Selene and Kane approaching them. As the trio walked up to them Selene chuckled.

"Oh wow. Who's *this* Magnolia?" Selene giggled as she looked Henry up and down with excited eyes. Initially, he was confused as to why Selene was eyeing him up so much. He soon remembered how he was not able to put his shirt back on when Magnolia pulled him out here, awkwardly crossed his arms across the middle of his body in an attempt at preserving some modesty. Selene laughed.

"This is Henry," Magnolia said. "He's the powerful Kin of Man we've been looking for."

Henry awkwardly waved at the three. Selene waved back with enthusiasm. Gabriel greeted him with a nod. Kane glared at him. Henry's eyes focused on him the most.

"Are you Gabriel?" Henry asked. Kane did not answer, holding his glare in silence. Henry scratched his head, not sure if he was more intimidated or confused by Kane.

"I'm Gabriel," Gabriel said. "I'm assuming Magnolia's told you about us?"

"Yeah, quite a lot actually," Henry chuckled.

"So, I'm assuming she's asked you to join us in making The Brew of Tranquillity?"

"She has."

"So then what's your answer?" asked Gabriel, eager as ever.

Henry rubbed his forehead in stress. "I'm not sure," he admitted. "I'm not sure at all."

Gabriel accepted his answer, nodding as he looked to the floor. Selene looked at Magnolia and groaned. Magnolia just shrugged back at her. Henry only looked at Kane, who was yet to say a single word yet and had not broken eye contact with the violent glares he sent his way.

"I know why he's not sure," Kane spoke up. "I knew the very second I laid eyes upon him."

Everyone's attention instantly diverted towards Kane.

"What are you talking about?" Gabriel asked.

Kane chose to answer Gabriel's question with actions instead of words. He lunged at Henry, grabbing at the skin on the back of his hip.

"What the hell are you doing?!" Henry asked as he pushed Kane off of him.

"What the hell is *that*?" asked Kane, pointing to the spot he was grasping at.

There, Henry sported a tattoo: the face of a beast, a mix of a line and an elk, with a sword and a drawn behind it. As soon as Gabriel and Magnolia saw the mark, their faces were coloured with shock. Henry hung his head in shame to avoid Magnolia's hurt gaze.

"What? What is that?" asked Selene, not understanding.

"A tattoo branded on those who have pledged themselves to The True One," Gabriel told her with a shaky voice. "The mark of Reyan's Vyre soldiers."

"No way!" gasped Selene, joining in on their outrage.

"Why do you have that, Henry?!" Magnolia asked in disbelief.

"I have a very reasonable explanation as to why," Henry assured her.

"Do you? Do you really?" asked Kane, voice laced with intimidation.

He closed the distance between him and Henry, squaring up to him in confrontation. He gradually heated his fists, smoke emerging from them.

"Look, you don't want to start a fight here," Henry warned him.

"Why, because you'll beat me?" scoffed Kane. "I don't think that's very likely."

"No, because the guards are trigger-happy with those whips and itching for an excuse to use them," said Henry, gesturing to a series of guards at the other side of the hallway. Just as suspected, the guards were watching a careful eye over the five of them, their hands hovering around their whips.

"I'm not scared of a couple of human guards," Kane scoffed.

"Well, *I am*, so let's not do this," said Henry.

"That's not *nearly* a good enough reason for me not to torch your dumbass right here and now," said Kane.

Henry sighed with exasperation. "Let's all go somewhere private to talk so I can explain myself. Okay?" he proposed. "Just don't cause a scene here."

Kane scowled at Henry, staring him up and down with contempt. Gabriel stepped in between the two tall men before a physical confrontation could erupt.

"Let's hear him out," he advised.

Kane looked over the rest of them to gauge their reactions. Magnolia gave him a soft nod whilst Selene simply shrugged. He grunted, accepting their decision, and backing away from Henry.

"Come with me," Henry sighed as walked back to the sleeping room. Gabriel gave a warning glare to Kane who rolled his eyes at him. The four of them followed Henry.

***

"How are the four new ones? Are they doing well?" Ms Alessandra George asked.

Her eye crystals shun, reflecting off glass beakers on the medic's desk she sat behind. Two asylum guards who stood across, heads down and arms folded.

"Not sure," said one of the guards.

"We'll keep a close eye on them," added the other.

"Good," said Alessandra. "Because I have a feeling that they'll cause us some problems here."

THE PASTS OF LANDS AND MEN

Henry sat atop his mattress as Gabriel, Magnolia, Kane, and Selene stood across from him in his dark cramped sleeping room, waiting for his explanation.

"Do any of you guys remember exactly what you were doing when the Second Great War between novatus and humans started?" he asked.

"Not really," answered Gabriel. Selene and Kane shook their heads.

"We all would have been pretty young back then," added Magnolia.

"Well, *I* do," said Henry. "Because it was the day when I got this."

Henry pointed towards the Vyre tattoo on the back of his hip with shame. All eyes in the room were fixed on the ink depiction of The True One.

"Here's the thing about being a Kin of Man. Unlike the rest of you guys we don't go around shooting out air or fire or lightning or vines or water, nor do I turn into a big massive beast. We're just good with weapons, plans and building things. The closest thing we have to anything supernatural is an accelerated healing factor which we can control. Meaning as long as we hide our birthmarks, we can hide that we are novatus. Even when our abilities go haywire." Henry explained.

"So, if you're a couple of human parents who happened to give birth to a novatus child and you find out he's off the class whose abilities can be hidden, you're going to try to take the chance. Mum may have wanted to ship me off but Dad convinced her that I could stay with them. That I could pose as a human and it'd all be fine."

Henry took another deep breath as he adjusted himself. The four of them listened attentively to his story, even Selene. Magnolia listened the closest of all.

"But that was easier said than done. Growing up as a kid around the neighbourhood I became very popular because I was so good at all the games. Whether it be simple play or intense sports matches, my Kin of Man abilities made me way better at everything than even some of the older kids were. Still, no one could figure out I was a novatus from that right? That's what I thought. And that's when I started to get carried away," Henry continued.

"It didn't catch up to me until one day I was play-fighting with some of the older kids in my neighbourhood. They wanted to play sword-fighting with these sharp sticks they found in the forest. They also wanted to finally teach me a lesson and beat me at something. Naturally, I beat all of them with ease which was pretty fun. What followed because of that wasn't."

Gabriel nudged Selene in the side, her attention starting to drift away from the story. Magnolia and Kane's attention could not have been yanked away from it if one tried, with Kane tightening his crossed arms.

"That led to the day my parents first met General Jiten, the man who used to lead the Vyre before Nathanael Reyan rose through the ranks. He had heard of how effortlessly good of a swordsman I seemed to be at such a tender young age. He was determined to groom me into the perfect soldier, to add to his ranks for the upcoming war. He was determined to convince them to let me join him," Henry continued. "My parents said no, obviously. Sending a kid who hadn't even seen his tenth birthday to war? That was crazy! But Jiten didn't care. He continued to press for weeks on end and my parents would continue to reject his request. It seemed nothing would get them to change their minds until Jiten revealed something. He knew I was secretly a novatus..."

"Oh no!" Selene gasped, having tuned into the story again.

"Oh no indeed," Henry laughed.

"Then what happened?" asked Magnolia. Henry cleared his throat to continue.

"Then Jiten took me with him to war. It was either that or he would expose my birthmark to everyone and have my parents lynched for harbouring an 'enemy of The True One.' Within weeks I was in one of his commander tents, receiving a Vyre soldier tattoo from him. He promised as long as I fought his war, he would help to keep my secret and protect my family back home. And so, I did. A great part of my childhood, hell most of my *life in general,* was spent on a series of war camps and battlefields."

Henry cradled his head for a moment. It panged with stress from reliving the memories. Magnolia sat next to him and put an arm around his shoulder. Henry brushed her off of him, insisting he was fine. He strengthened his resolve and sought to continue onwards.

"It was horrible. Fighting for the side of the humans, being forced to kill what I knew were my people from a very young age. But at least after the war was won, I could go back home to my family and forget it all happened right?"

"Right?" Selene repeated hopefully. Henry shook his head at her.

"Wrong! A year and a half ago, I came back to see that my parents fled without telling me. And on top of that, they had ratted me out to save themselves!" Henry exclaimed. "So, after almost a decade of gruelling war, I didn't just have no family to come back to, but an entire village I grew up in hated me, shunned me, and shooed me out! I've spent the past year running and hiding! I knew I couldn't fit back into human society and I couldn't bear to show my face at any novatus shelter in fear that someone might recognise me from the battlefield! I had nowhere to go until I was forced to come *here*."

Henry waved around the dark and shabby, practically empty 'sleeping room' of his that they all stayed in, gesturing at the Asylum as a whole. The others gazed upon him with a newfound sympathy in both their eyes and hearts. Magnolia especially.

"So yes. I have the mark of Vyre stuck on my body forever. But believe me, I'm just as annoyed about it as you are..." Henry finished. He glared at the rest of them, Kane specifically. Kane uncrossed his arms, his body shifting with awkward guilt.

"I suppose I understand now," he grumbled reluctantly. "Apologies for considering you a traitor to our people and all."

"It's alright. I'm glad you guys can understand," sighed Henry. "And I hope it can also explain why even though I'd like to help you make The Brew of Tranquillity, I can't."

"But why not?" asked Gabriel.

"Me? A person who fought and was hated by both sides of the aisle?" he chuckled. "I have no business trying to protect anything, never mind save the world or my people."

The other four shared unsure looks with one another, no one knowing what to say to him. The only one not at a loss for words was Magnolia. "That's not true Henry. In fact, I think it's quite the opposite."

"How?" he scoffed.

"Because I understand you," Magnolia told him. "I might not know what it's like to feel like a traitor to your people, but I do know what it's like to be shunned and disregarded by your family and the people you grew up with."

"You do?" Henry asked.

Magnolia inhaled a deep breath through her nose and sat down right next to Henry.

"Do you know Roosevelt Thorne, Grand Leader of the Third Kingdom?" she asked. Henry nodded his head. Magnolia did not say anything for a moment, grinding her teeth as if to endure an immense struggle to get the words out. "He's-"

"Magnolia. You don't have to talk about this if you don't want to," Gabriel interrupted her with assurance. Magnolia shook her head at him.

"It's pretty much always been an open secret to a lot of people anyway, so I might as well open it further," sighed Magnolia. She turned back to Henry and looked him deep in the eye. "Roosevelt Thorne is my father, which makes me the former princess of the Third Kingdom."

Henry's jaw dropped. "Oh wow," he gasped. His face shared the same expression with Selene who was not yet privy to this information and Kane who had heard rumours of it back at the shelter but never confirmed by Magnolia herself.

"You're part of one of the four royal families?!" Selene asked in shocked excitement.

"Not anymore," Magnolia sighed. "I left the family and the kingdom as a preteen."

"You're a child of one of the Grand Leaders *and* a novatus? I'm surprised you didn't leave even earlier," said Henry.

"I was a late bloomer, so I spent most of my childhood completely unaware I was a novatus," Magnolia explained. "Do you want to know what happened the week my birthmark finally formed and novatus abilities kicked in?"

Henry nodded with hesitance. Magnolia gritted her teeth together again, trying her damnedest to push through the pain and finish what she had started.

"My father held a celebration throughout the main square of the Third Kingdom to commemorate him 'plucking a weed' from his family! He wanted to make sure that the people of his kingdom knew he did not know I was a novatus and that he was completely against my being born!" she cried. "And so, the guards of my very own castle, on bequest of my *very own father*, paraded me around the kingdom, allowing anyone and everyone to mock, jeer at, spit on and *beat* me for days on end! Then when it was all over, he banished me not just from the family but from the entire Third Kingdom, never to return!"

Magnolia could hardly contain herself any longer, bursting into a fit of tears the second she finished telling her life story. She was immediately comforted from both sides with Henry placing a rubbing arm on her shoulder and Selene jumping over to hug her.

"Thank you, Selene," Magnolia muttered as she smiled at her. Selene smiled with a warm genuine smile back in place of her usually irreverent one. Gabriel nodded his head as he looked into Magnolia's eyes deeply. Kane looked to the floor to avoid the feelings that were being thrown around the room right at the moment.

"That's horrible," said Henry.

"It is. But it's why I need to see this Brew of Tranquillity mission through. Because of what happened to me, I struggle with thinking about my worth as a person *and* as a novatus. Just like you," said Magnolia with a bold resolve. "That's why we both need to do this. To prove ourselves *wrong*. That we do mean something and that we can make a change for our people!"

Henry could not take his eyes off Magnolia, simultaneously, saddened, uplifted, and mesmerised by her and all she had said. Kane looked up from the floor, nodding emphatically in agreement with Magnolia's sentiments. Gabriel joined him in nodding, as did Selene. As he looked around at all their faces in the room, Henry seemed like he was quickly being convinced, yet was not yet completely reeled in. That was when Gabriel stepped forward.

"My past and my story may be vastly different to yours, but like Magnolia, I can relate to you in some way," said Gabriel. "The mistakes I made when I was younger, the actions I took, they made me feel like

I did a disservice to my people too. But together we're all going to rectify any and all things we may have gone through in the past. *Together.*"

Henry looked over all their faces. All of them were coloured with an immensely welcoming glow, even Kane's. Henry smiled. "Okay, you've got me," he sighed with a chuckle. "How could I possibly say no to being your Kin of Man now?"

Gabriel's tense shoulders dropped with relief. His mouth stretched into the widest of Cheshire-esque smiles as he offered Henry a handshake. Magnolia watched in delight as Henry stood up from the bed to accept Gabriel's hand for the firmest of handshakes. A deal was made.

"There is one issue with me joining you guys, though."

"What is it?"

"If we're going to be travelling all the way to the Fourth Kingdom, we're going to have to get out of this asylum first."

"It's fine. I've already thought up a plan for how we can leave without Alessandra finding out," Kane told the two of them.

"You have?" Gabriel asked.

"Yeah, he's good. He came up with the plan for us to get in here in the first place. Isn't that right Kane-Kang?" Selene said. Kane kissed his teeth at her.

"When did you come up with a plan?" asked Magnolia.

"Whilst you guys were sharing sob stories," Kane answered mockingly, to which she rolled her eyes. "By the way Henry, can we sleep here for the night?"

"Of course. My staying room is your staying room," said Henry.

"Good. I'll have plenty of time to explain the plan and plenty more time to prepare," Kane said. "Tomorrow morning, we'll break out.

NOW LEAVING RECKONEN ASYLUM

The next morning, the five woke up brimming with excitement and bravado, determined to break out of the asylum without a hitch. They spent the entirety of the night prior discussing the details of their escape. They discussed exactly how they were going to put it into action and leave freely with their new Kin of Man on their team and embark to find their Kin of Beasts. Led by Kane, the five of them marched out of Henry's staying room and into the halls, ready to implement his plan.

Though as soon as they stepped, they were halted in their tracks and confronted by ten or so guards. The guards glowered down at the group with their hands firmly on whips.

"Ms George needs to see you all," one said. "Now."

The group looked around at each other, confused as to what to do next. Gabriel looked to Kane for an answer, but Kane had nothing. The group obliged, following the guards.

***

The guards ushered them into the pungent-smelling, shelve-surrounded, potion and instrument-cluttered medical room that was Ms Alessandra George's office. Alessandra sat behind the desk, eye crystals glinting and smiling with amusement as she took in the group.

"Oh wow, it seems you've all become fast friends with Mr Popular," she said, gesturing to Henry. "How nice is that-"

"They said you wanted to see us?" Kane interrupted with impatience. "What for?"

Alessandra smiled warmly. "I just wanted to make sure you're all doing okay, that's all," she said, her voice rife with mischief. "Are the facilities up to your standards?"

"They are." lied Gabriel. Magnolia, and Selene nodded in corroboration with him. "We all managed to settle in quite nicely and had a good sleep."

"So, you're enjoying your stay here?" asked Alessandra.

"Yes, very much so," Gabriel lied.

"So then why do you plan on escaping?" Alessandra asked.

The colour in Gabriel's face drained within an instant. He stood there; teeth clenched. He looked over to the rest of the group. Each one of them froze, holding the same uncertainty on their faces. Alessandra laughed.

"'How did she know?' I bet you're thinking... because I'm a clever bastard, that's how," she said laughing. "And because I could read the looks on your faces. Those are the faces people make when they're caught in the act."

Alessandra gestured at each of their faces. The five novatus just stood there, still unclear as to what their next move should be. Alessandra shook her head at them and smirked, much to the amusement of the asylum guards. She leaned forward over her desk, her eye crystals glinting with a dangerous light.

"But before you try to escape, I'd like to show you something."

The group waited with bated breath as she reached underneath her desk. The asylum owner rifled underneath the cluttered space under her desk and pulled out a heavy bag. With a flick of her wrist, she emptied the contents onto the table. Out dropped the body of a dead young novatus, whipped in half and with a face destroyed. The group squirmed with shock and disgust as they looked at the jagged whip marks scorched in the flesh.

Alessandra pointed at the corpse. "This is what happens to people who try to escape my asylum," she said, her voice low and menacing. "Either this or they get sent to The Farm."

"The Farm?" Kane asked.

"The Farm," she repeated. "It's a little project I'm conducting with Reyan. I send 'uncooperative' novatus there, and they work like slaves with their arms clamped up. We break down and use them until their abilities are heightened, then they are shipped off to Reyan. I get to study novatus more at the height of their abilities then he gets more novatus to take and feed to The True One. It's a very mutually beneficial deal we've got going on."

The disappointment and disgust the group felt upon hearing her explanation was palpable. Smoke formed within Kane's clenched fists and Gabriel's eyes flashed with anger.

"Do you want to end up at The Farm?" Alessandra asked, chuckling sadistically. She was met with five hostile novatus stares of silent anger and disgust. "No? Then I suggest you stay put."

She leaned back in her chair, a satisfied smirk playing at the corners of her lips. The fire within Kane's hands burned with rising rage. He had heard enough.

Kane over the desk, his eyes burning as bright as his hands as he charged towards Alessandra. Before he could make contact, three guards tackled him to the ground, whipping him with their metal chains. Magnolia reacted quickly, unleashing her vines to trap the other guards to the wall. Henry retrieved a hidden knife from his pocket, throwing it with precision at the guard closest to him, the knife embedding itself in the unfortunate thug's skull. The other guards hesitated for a moment, watching the building chaos. Gabriel seized the opportunity, manipulating the air in his vicinity. He knocked Alessandra back with a powerful gust, sending her crashing into the shelves on the back wall. Quick on her feet, Selene created a wave of dark energy that swept Kane up and away from the guards, who were still trying to subdue him.

"Fuck Kane's plan! We're doing mine!" she shouted as she did so.

"What's your plan?" Magnolia asked, observing the chaos unfolding around them.

Selene enlarged the wave of dark energy she engulfed Kane in, enveloping Gabriel, Magnolia, and Henry within it too.

"Hold on tight!" she ordered as she leapt on the dark energy wave her friends were encapsulated in. With that, Selene surfed atop the dark energy she had created, moving at incredible speeds as they burst out of Ms George's office and into the main halls. As they tore through the establishment, they knocked past crowds of asylum members and guards, making efforts to grab at and whip them. Not a single person was could keeping up.

Finally, they reached the main door, heavily guarded by several armed men. Selene used her abilities to collect all the water from the general area, creating a massive wave that knocked the door down with ease. As they burst out of the asylum's main entrance, they crash-landed on the side street they had first seen the asylum from. Though groggy and disoriented from the chaotic ride, they were quick to get back up.

"Crap," grunted Henry, looking up to see several guards from outside of the gate chasing them.

"Leg it!" Selene screamed. And so, they did, running with the utmost haste through the side streets. The hounding guards bellowed at them, their voices growing louder as they cracked their whips.

A short while later, Alessandra and her head guards stepped out of the asylum building. Ms George scanned the area around them, her sharp gaze taking in every detail as she rubbed her chin with deep thought.

"Where could they have gone?" she muttered to herself.

The guards exchanged unknowing glances.

"Should we hunt them down and bring them back here?" one asked hesitantly.

Alessandra shifted her gaze to him, her expression inscrutable.

"Hunt them down, but don't bring them back here," she said slowly.

"Why?" he asked.

Alessandra giggled. "Just initiate Plan Three-Five-One," she ordered.

***

The five novatus panted wildly as they ran down another cobbled side street, urgently searching for a way out of the city. Their hearts raced as they heard the sound of chariots approaching them from around the corner.

"We have to go another way!" Magnolia exclaimed.

They backtracked and ran down another area. They passed by another street and headed down its alleyway, but just as they entered, they were intercepted by another group of guards riding a remarkably fast horse-drawn carriage.

"Another way!" Kane exclaimed. But when the group ran out of this alleyway and onto another, more chariots and carriages blocked their paths.

"Another way," Gabriel sighed dejectedly as they repeated the process.

The group kept having to run down different side streets to escape from the intercepting chariots and carriages over and over and *over* again. That was until they found an opening that led them into a forest of wooded trees.

"Alright, this *has* to be the way!" Selene said as they bounded towards the opening.

As they ran into the forest, a strange wobbling sound vibrated through the air. A sound that all five of them were too busy thinking about evading capture to even notice.

The five sprinted deep into the forest, rushing through the winding paths, passing by dozens of trees. As they ran deeper into the forest, Selene glanced back to check the status of their assailants.

"They're not chasing us anymore!" she notified them with a shout.

The group finally stopped running, panting, and gasping as they collected their breath again.

***

As the five of them relaxed by the trees, Henry took notice of the flora and fauna that surrounded them. He inspected the area, noticing how the trees were mismatched all over the forest. Only a few looked like they belonged in a forest. Most looked like they belonged in a jungle. Some had black leaves and grey bushes. The further Henry inspected, the further his suspicions grew. He looked to the sky to see a transparent wobbly barrier filling the skies above them. Henry cursed himself under his breath for having not noticed it before. His suspicions had been confirmed.

"Those damn guards tricked us." He grumbled.

"What's wrong?" asked Magnolia, looking at him nervously.

"We just made a big mistake," Henry said, his face pale.

"How so?" asked Kane.

Henry rubbed his forehead with stress.

"We just accidentally trapped ourselves in the Prisoners Forest."

THE DREADED FOREST OF PRISONERS

"Why do we spend so much time here?" asked a Vyre soldier. He stood by the rocky shore of the mountain's river as Reyan once again, bathed in it. "Shouldn't we return to our duties?"

"My being in this river is what aids our duties," said Reyan. He showcased the skin of his arms to his soldier, stretching it out and twisting it around to flaunt its hardening glow. The novatus aren't the only ones allowed to have power..."

"Oh right, of course. Sorry for questioning you sir," the soldier apologised.

Reyan scoffed at the man with a soft chuckle.

"I want you and the others to be ready by the time I finish bathing," he told him.

"Are we finally going back to hunting down more novatus for The True One's illness?" asked the hopeful soldier.

"Not quite. In light of some recent news, we're required back in the First Kingdom," Reyan said. "Certain individuals need to be put in their place."

***

Evening time came and passed into the night, yet the sounds of the Prisoners Forest only grew louder. It had been hours since Henry had informed them of the mistake, they made in coming here, the regret gradually sinking in.

The five of them sat precariously on the sturdy branches of the tallest, widest oak tree, its leaves were the closest thing to shelter they could find all night. From high above, they looked down upon the constantly unfolding horrors of the forest below.

A Kin of Skies prisoner with wild coarse matted hair, summoned the air around her, creating a massive cyclone and spinning constantly until she lost consciousness. She would pass out, wake up, and do it all over again in a seemingly unbreakable pathological loop.

A Kin of Land prisoner caused havoc from afar, a smile on his jagged stone-like face. Using his earth manipulation abilities he created massive fissures in the ground beneath him, causing trees to topple and the forest floor to quake. His movements were slow and deliberate enjoying the destruction he was causing. He cackled maniacally as he tore through the forest, sending rocks and boulders tumbling down hillsides.

A Kin of Sun prisoner with skin as white as snow, generated a piercing light over and over. She directed the light into her own eyes, purposefully attempting to blind herself.

A Kin of Man prisoner broke bark from a tree, whittling it into a sword as he ate meat with a group of comrades. When his whittling was done, he used this sword to stab his comrades, then himself.

Finally, a Kin of Moon prisoner with dark, mottled skin manipulated the water around her. She would drag it through the dirt, drink it, throw it up, then collecting more from the rivers to repeat the process.

Selene watched these prisoners all across the forest with morbid curiosity. She could not determine whether she was more fascinated or terrified.

"The Prisoner's Forest," she muttered, chuckling to Henry who sat on the branch next to her. He paid no attention to her nor the sights she was directing him to. She shrugged, looking away from the scenes below and towards a higher branch.

"How are you guys getting on?"

On the branch above them were Gabriel, Kane, and Magnolia, standing on the highest vantage point inside the forest. Gabriel zapped lightning into the sky, hitting the barrier in an effort to break it. Kane joined him in trying to create a hole in the barrier, shooting fire at the same spot as Magnolia did the same with wild pounding vines. Despite their gruelling efforts, the barrier was just as unmoved and undented as when they had first started trying to break it hours ago.

"Not good," wheezed Gabriel as he and Magnolia stopped their efforts.

"Ms George made the barrier using the farmed abilities of many powerful novatus," said Henry. "This is where she puts the prisoners with abilities too reckless and behaviour too unpredictable for her and her guards to control. It's designed not to break very easily."

191

"So, this is no use, right?" asked Magnolia. Henry nodded in confirmation. She sighed. "Not what I wanted to hear."

Gabriel, Kane, and Magnolia sat back down on their branch, tired from the constant use of their abilities. It appeared as if the five of them would remain in the trees for hours more.

"You know, if this is how I knew things were going to go, I think I should have just stayed in the Asylum." Henry joked.

"Very funny," scoffed Magnolia, to Henry's amusement. "We'll get out of here eventually; we just need to keep cool heads and figure out a way how."

"You know, it's technically Kane's fault we're here," said Selene.

"Last time I checked you were the stupid fuck whose escape plan landed us here." retorted Kane.

"I only did that because your plan failed! Sorry that I had to enprovise, *Kane.*"

"That's not how you say improvise, *dumbass.*"

"I'll say whatever words however I want *plan-failer.*"

Selene blew a raspberry at Kane immaturely. He scowled at her, shaking his head.

"Oi, Mr Kin of Man," he called out to Henry.

"Yes?"

"Isn't your novatus class supposed to be good at creating weird ingenious plans?"

"Uh, yeah. I guess."

"Then how come you haven't come up with one the whole time we've been here?"

Henry lowered his gaze away from Kane at the top branch and across the horizon. He looked past all of the deranged prisoners who ran about and towards the heart of the forest where there was a gap in the trees.

"There *is* one idea that sprung to mind a while ago," Henry admitted. "And if we somehow managed to pull it off, we'd kill two birds with one stone."

"What do you mean?"

"We'd be able to not just escape, but escape having recruited the Kin of Beasts we need."

Gabriel's ears instantly perked up. "Why didn't you tell us before, then?!" he asked.

"Because it's quite strange, very risky and probably too dangerous," said Henry.

"Our entire mission is strange, risky and dangerous," said Magnolia. "So, you might as well say it."

Henry abruptly scaled down the tree, landing on the forest floors. He began collecting as many odd sticks and fallen branches as he could find.

"What are you doing?" Selene asked.

He ignored her as he formed the branches into a massive pile to work on. Using only a small knife retrieved from underneath his trousers, skilful hands, and a little ingenuity, Henry crafted at superhuman speeds. The four watched him carefully as he used his Kin of Man abilities to create a fully-function polished cannon out of wood. Henry pushed his hands out to showcase his creation. The other four scaled themselves down the tree and onto the forest floor to get a closer look, marvelling at it in approbation.

"Woah, cool!" Selene exclaimed.

"Impressive," Gabriel commented.

"Very impressive," Magnolia agreed.

"Yes, very good," Kane scoffed. "But how does your art project help us break the barrier?"

Henry grew giddy with excitement as he glanced at his creation.

"When you, Gabriel, and Magnolia were using your abilities to attack the barrier it didn't even leave a dent. I guessed it was because although your abilities were powerful, they are too blunt and lacking in raw force to break the barrier. Alessandra probably designed it to be that way," explained Henry. "But, using all four of your elemental abilities as fuel, we can shoot a concentrated attack from his cannon at the barrier which should be able to make a hole in it of at least a few inches."

"That's great! Problem solved!" Selene celebrated.

"Not quite," said Magnolia. "How are we going to escape through only a small hole?"

"And how does this relate to our finding of the Kin of Beasts?" asked Gabriel.

Henry scratched at the crown of his wavy blond hair.

"Yeah, that's where the stupidly strange, risky and dangerous part comes in," he admitted reluctantly. "It sounds weird, but my plan only works if we escape via riding the back of a Kin of Beasts as they leaps towards the hole we'll create. With its structural integrity being compromised it could potentially be torn through. So, we need to find a powerful Kin of Beast who can use their claws to do said tearing."

"An odd plan, but it's most definitely worth at least seeing through," said Gabriel. "Only issue is finding a powerful enough Kin of Beasts."

"They're the rarest novatus class remember," Kane reminds Henry.

"Finding one is easy, that's not the issue," said Henry.

"Then what is the issue?" asked Magnolia.

"Dealing with the Kin of Beasts themselves," Henry said ominously. He was met with a series of confused and concerned looks from the others as they waited for elaboration.

"Have any of you heard of Eva Lander?" he asked. Again, he was met with concerned blank faces coupled with shaking heads. Henry sighed as he picked up his wooden cannon with him. He gestured at the other four to follow him as he ventured deeper into the forest.

"Well, you're about to meet her."

After half an hour of the five walking through the forest, avoiding the deranged prisoners and unruly elements that surrounded them, Henry finally led them to their destination. They arrived at the part of the forest he had been gazing at over the horizon. This part of the Prisoner's Forest was different from the others. The trees were sparser around this area where no prisoner dared to come. Except for one.

A large humanoid lion slept in a wide crater of a pit in the middle of the area. Dozens of feet tall, the creature curled up within itself, snoring away.

"Is *that* Eva Lander?" Selene asked. Henry nodded.

The group observed with wonder as Henry brought them only a few metres away from the slumbering beast. With every third snore, the novatus would transform from a beastly lion-person dozens of feet tall to a petite brunette young woman barely over five-feet tall. The group were captured by a wicked fascination as they watched her sleep. Gabriel and Kane most of all.

"Thirteen years," Henry muttered.

"Sorry, what did you say?" asked Selene.

"For the past thirteen or so years, Eva has been one of the most dangerously infamous novatus the Prisoner's Forest has in its captivity," explained Henry.

Gabriel seemed baffled by this revelation. "Thirteen years?! But she looks as young as we are!" he exclaimed "Was she imprisoned as a little child?" asked Gabriel.

"She was," answered Henry.

"So, she would have been here even before The Second Great War?" Kane asked.

"That's what happens when your abilities make you too hard to kill and too risky to deal with," Henry sighed.

"But what could a child so young do to get thrown in here?" asked Magnolia.

Henry looked at the others through the corner of his eye.

"Eat their own mother," Henry answered. The others reacted with shock and disgust. Except for Kane, who somehow seemed even more fascinated.

"She ate her mother?!" Selene asked in outrage. "What, like on purpose?!"

"I don't know," said Henry. "All I know is that her lion transformation abilities are intense. There's a reason barely anyone comes over to this part of the forest."

The shock and disgust on Gabriel, Selene and Magnolia's faces mixed with pale fear.

"Perhaps when she finds out we plan on finally freeing her, she won't be hostile?" Magnolia suggested

"Yeah, but we have to wake her up first," said Henry.

"And I'm guessing that's the risky and dangerous part?" asked Gabriel. Henry nodded.

The five stared at Eva who continued to transform in and out of her lion form as she slept.

***

Cold, injured and beaten down both physically and mentally, Enzo Caelestis was a far cry from the powerful clan leader he had once been. The wounds he sustained from the Battle at the Castle of Debris were still aching and the shame he felt for having betrayed Kane by leaving him on the battlefield was still fresh.

Enzo's body shook as he huddled within the confines of a damp cave, his eyes darting about the darkened space. Despite his current condition, he had determination in his eyes. He did not yet consider himself down for the count. Far from it.

He planned on finally leaving the cave when he got healthier, planning to regroup and strategise with whatever surviving novatus he could find in the land. He planned on getting his revenge on Kaymore and The First Kingdom, once and for all…

…but just as Enzo was considering his options and running them through his head, he felt a jarring impact strike the back of it. He cried out in agony as he experienced the immense pressure of a spear being driven into his skull. The world spun as he collapsed to the ground, dead.

Nathanael Reyan and a dozen Vyre soldiers were outside the cave, standing atop a hill a few miles away. With another spear in his hand, Reyan shook his head and scoffed.

***

"So how are we going to do this? Hmm?" Selene asked. Her, Gabriel, Henry, and Magnolia were huddled together contemplating how they would wake Eva as her snores echoed in the background. "We could use one of our abilities to tap on her shoulders and dodge away before she attacks us?"

"Maybe," considered Magnolia. "How fast is she?"

"Very fast," Henry answered.

"Be more specific," asked Gabriel. "How fast would we have to be to avoid her attacks if she wakes up hostile?"

"Very very fast," Henry said.

"That's helpful," Magnolia snarked.

"This is my first time seeing her in person!" Henry defended. "I'm not sure as to how we should plan to wake her up, I just know that we should."

"Maybe Kane the Planner has another plan for us," scoffed Selene.

"Where did heaven go?" asked Gabriel.

The four turned around to see Kane approaching Eva in her pit with a wicked smile on his face and an intense look in his eyes. Gabriel's eyes widened, his fear and panic felt by the rest of the group as they watched Kane.

"Kane! Don't-"

Before Gabriel could finish his sentence, Kane had already generated an enormous ball of light energy and thrown it at Eva. The bright light attack smacked into Eva's face, waking her up.

The group watched in horror as Eva roared, transforming into an even larger humanoid lion creature of epic monstrous proportions. She unleashed her awakened fury on the group, the earth beneath them trembling and cracking under the weight of her giant feline body.

The group did their best to defend themselves and try to quell her impending rampage. Gabriel summoned a gust of wind to try and knock Eva off balance, while Magnolia summoned vines to restrain her and Selene summoned water to create a barrier between Eva and the rest of the group. But the humanoid lion simply roared and charged through it, tearing the barrier apart with her strong, beastly claws. Henry revealed a hidden knife and tried to stab Eva, who swatted him away with a powerful swipe of her paw, sending him tumbling across the ground. Gabriel conjured up a spinning cyclone and prepared to attack her with it, but Lion Eva simply roared and charged through it, tearing through the barrier. The attacks came and came, but nothing could stop Eva from swatting them away, bringing down the trees around them.

The only one who did not fight was Kane, who stood calmly to the side, watching the chaos unfold with a smile on his face. Lion Eva took notice of his lack of fear and inaction, seeking him specifically.

"Hello," Kane greeted her with a casual smirk on his face.

Lion Eva roared down at him fiercely. She leered over him, her jaw unhinged and threatening to eat him whole.

"I said *hello*," Kane repeated casually. "Don't you wish to speak with me?"

Much to the surprise of everyone else, Eva listened, morphing back down to her human form.

"What do you people want?!" she demanded. "You trying to hunt me or something?!"

Kane chuckled. "If I wanted to kill you, I would've done so whilst you slept," he said. "I just wanted to get to know you. Powerful novatus should stick together, wouldn't you agree?"

Eva scoffed. "You don't look very powerful to me," she said, eyeing him suspiciously.

"You'd be surprised," Kane laughed.

Eva was not as amused. "Just leave me alone!" she shouted at him. "I'm not in the mood to fight!"

"I told you; I just want to get to know you," Kane replied with a smile.

Eva gritted her teeth in anger. "Well, you can get to know the dirt!" she shouted.

Within the blink of an eye, she returned to her lion form. The forceful impact of her powerful paws swiftly struck Kane's head, knocking him out cold.

"Aw crap!" Selene exclaimed.

The others panicked as Eva resumed her attack on them, thrashing about, and destroying the earth around her with her heavy fists and roaring out of her many-toothed snarling jaws. The group struggled to defend themselves from her, running further down the forest as she pushed them back with swiping claw attacks.

Kane remained unconscious to the side. As he lay asleep with his face in the forest dirt, the inner workings of his subconscious mind took him far away from the present, in place and time...

THE TROUBLING CHILDHOOD OF KANE KEAHI

Five years. That was how long Kane Keahi had been on the Earth when he and his father, Kal, had fled their original land together. Cuts and bruises littered both of their bodies and depression marked their faces as they washed up on the shores of a First Kingdom Island.

"Come on son, let's go," Kal said as he cradled his arms around his child.

"Okay Dad," Kane whimpered, his voice high, shaky, and scared. The two of them walked further on looking for any form of shelter.

Kane and his father made sure to keep their heads low as they travelled through the land. The last thing the two novatus needed was to be spotted by any humans. They spent weeks on end moving from place to place to avoid this. They spent days hiding in the woods and nights sleeping on the streets of the outskirts of abandoned towns.

They spent afternoons trekking through the coarse beaches and evenings in whatever abandoned buildings they could find.

Using their Kin of Sun abilities, they were able to hunt for food and warm themselves at night. Though this barely worked to alleviate their suffering. The unfortunate father and son duo made sure to never stay hidden in one place for too long, for fear of being discovered by humans. Usually, they were careful, but at times, they were not careful enough.

One night, the pair of them had been found in what they thought was an abandoned barn. Truly, it belonged to an unscrupulous farmer who caught them early in the morning, mere minutes before they planned to move again. Though the farmer was a coarse-faced and lecherous-looking man, he defied both of their expectations. He did not try to kill them, hurt them, or even think of notifying the Vyre about them. He simply smirked at them, opportunity shining in his eyes.

"How about we strike a deal?" the farmer asked Kal.

Later, he and his small group of leering workers looked over the two novatus. The head farmer had brought the two onto the field of dead grass to show the other workers on the farm the novatus he had found. The pair were stricken with fear as they saw the maliciously snickering humans in front of them.

"What kind of deal?" Kal asked timidly as Kane hid behind him.

"My workers bust our asses on this farm every day and let me tell you we're damn tired of it," groaned the head farmer, to which the others murmured in corroboration. "So instead, from now on, you're going to do all the work around here in exchange for us *not* choosing to send you both straight to the Vyre. Okay?"

"Okay…" said Kal, nodding as his body shook with fear. The other farmers smiled with lecherous glee as Kane peeked out from behind his father.

"Fair warning though, you're going to be worked to the bone for the low price of nothing!" guffawed the head farmer, his other workers chuckling too.

"Like…like a slave?" Kane asked, his voice quaking to no end.

The head farmer smirked with malevolence in his eyes. He crouched down to speak to Kane on his level. "Yes, little boy," he laughed. "Like a slave."

***

Kane and his father were given a 'room' to stay in - a manure-covered corner of the barn next to stacks of hay and rusted old farming tools. That was where they were to wake up day in and day out to perform their daily duties.

Life on the farm was rough for the father and son. Their workdays on the farm would start as early as three in the morning where they were tasked with digging tunnels and tending to crops. If even as many as *one* set of crops died or one mistake was made in the tunnel, then the pair of them would receive a form of 'physical reprimanding' from the farmer. Then, they had to water the fields, harvest the produce, fix broken equipment, fertilise the crops by hand, deal with pests and tidy up the land, the barn, and the farmhouse until the sunset. Again, any small mistake made when completing these tasks was met with many rounds of physical reprimanding.

This could range from a simple beating delivered by all of the farmers at once to lashes from a whip to iron branding on their skin to the seldom pulling out of fingernails. Considering how often they were reprimanded, one would assume that the farmers would take it easier on Kane, a child barely half a decade old. The reality was quite the opposite. If the anything, farmers enjoyed dolling out these physical punishments on Kane more than they did on his father. Kal could only watch with timidity as his son was doled out twice the punishment day in and day out.

"Why do we have to do this?" a teary-eyed Kane asked one day, laying on a bed of hay next to his father. He rubbed his back, sore from a day's worth of hard labour and beatings.

"We made a deal with them, son," sighed Kal. "We can't leave now."

"Can't we just use our abilities to escape?" Kane asked.

With a snap of his finger, he created a small wisp of fire. Just as quickly as Kane generated the fire, Kal extinguished it with one clasping hand. The other hand struck his son across the face with a vicious backhand slap. Kane stumbled back in shock as his father pointed an accusatory finger in his face.

"You need to be more damn careful son!" Kal exclaimed in a desperate panic.

Kane quivered as he saw the potent fear and anger in his dads' eyes. "But-"

"It may be awful and tiresome, but staying here gets us proper food in our bellies and a roof over our heads. *Without* us having to run and hide and fear being caught on human land!" Kal rambled, interrupting him. "Do NOT ruin this for us! Okay?"

"Okay," Kane whimpered, rubbing the mark his father's blow left on his face.

That was how they lived their lives for the following three years. In constant suffering on the farm.

Almost every day felt the same for Kane. He woke up early, was worked to the bone all day, abused by the farmers for his mistakes, reprimanded by his father for even considering the notion of escaping, then cry himself to bed to get what sleep he could until the next day.

Up, work, abused, reprimanded, cry to sleep. Up, work, abused, reprimanded, cry to sleep. Up, work, abused, reprimanded, cry to sleep. Each day of pain blended into the next until one day, something snapped.

Early that morning, the head farmer opened the barn in which the father and son slept, ready to force them into another day of gruelling work. "Rise and shine-"

The farmer stopped in the middle of his sentence. What he saw in the barn that morning, had left him utterly speechless.

Kal Keahi lay on a bed of hay, the skin on his face burnt off. The farmer's mouth squirmed, stomach churned, unable to take his eyes off of the sight.

"He's dead," said the voice of a young child behind him. He swivelled to see Kane standing behind him menacingly. The look he saw on Kane's face, was not one any child should have held.

"Back down boy," he ordered, the shakiness in his voice exposing the fear in his heart.

"No," Kane disobeyed bluntly.

"Back down before I give you another round of 'reprimanding'," threatened the farmer. Kane chose to do the opposite, closing the distance between them. The farmer's distress doubled.

"I said back down you little cunt! I'll-"

With a flurry of fire, Kane produced the hottest flames he could muster from the palm of his hands. The head farmer screamed in agonising pain as Kane burnt the skin off of his flesh and the flesh off of his bones. The louder the farmer screamed as his body melted in excruciating torment, the more delight Kane felt, grinning from ear to ear as his heart beat faster. In a mere matter of seconds, the head farmer was nothing more than a pile of ash. A pile of ash Kane spat on and kicked around, laughing all the while.

"What the hell's going on here?" asked another one of the farmers. Kane turned around to see the rest of the workers of the farm all pour into the barn. His gleeful smile widened as they came close.

Hours later, Kane left the farm for the first time in three years. As he left the farmland with a smile on his face, every inch of land from the fields to the barn burnt in bright hot flames. Smoke lifted itself off of Kane's twitching fingertips as he casually left the scene of his crime.

He was now alone. A young kid forced to travel throughout the First Kingdom with no one to accompany or protect him. Yet he did not feel fearful. He felt free.

***

Kane woke up in the present, picking his face off of the forest floors. His eyes scoured the area as he slowly recalled what had been occurring before he was knocked out. As he stood to his feet, he looked in the distance to see a cleared path of destroyed trees and charred bushes. Down the path he saw Gabriel, Magnolia, Selene, and Henry still struggling to defend themselves as Lion Eva rampaged on. With a grin on his face, Kane heated a large fireball in his hands and marched his way back into battle.

JASON BOJE

KIN OF KIN

Kane threw himself fully into the fight against Eva, deftly evading her attacks while unleashing torrents of fire in her direction. Unlike the others, who fought with caution and wariness, Kane fought with passion and lust. He irreverently faced Lion Eva as if he were playing a game, taunting her in between attacks.

"Is it true that you killed your mother?" he yelled as he shot a flurry of fire towards her.

Gabriel, Henry, Magnolia, and Selene shared a worried glance with Kane before exchanging glances amongst themselves.

"What is he doing?!" Henry asked quietly.

"What are you doing?" Magnolia mouthed worriedly. Kane paid no mind to them whatsoever, his attention focused on laughing at Eva's furious roars.

"Not only did you murder your mother, but you ate her too. I have to say, that's quite the uniquely cruel crime," he taunted.

Lion Eva bounded towards him on all fours, the ground quaking from impact. The others struggled to keep her at bay as Kane continued his barrage of insults.

"Very *very* uniquely cruel!" he yelled as he dodged another one of Eva's swiped-paw attacks. "How could you do something like that?!"

Eva's actions grew increasingly erratic as she tried to assail Kane. Multiple times she saw herself only inches away from succeeding in decapitating him only to knock down a tree instead.

"Kane, what exactly is your plan here?!" asked a worried Gabriel as he formed air walls and gas cyclones to slow Eva down. The wind attacks failed, Eva mindlessly swatting them away. She continued her pursuit towards Kane who welcomed her forward.

"It's because you can't control your abilities, isn't it?" Kane said in a softer voice. Eva clawed at him, a blow he deflected with a streak of flames. "But that doesn't mean you should be punished, beaten, and abused for life, does it?"

Lion Eva's furry brow furrowed as she looked down at Kane.

"How dare they trap you in a place like this?" he exclaimed.

Eva's sweaty, panting, rampaging anger slowly subsided, morphing into a confused curiosity.

"It doesn't mean you should constantly suffer for one mistake!" Kane cried.

Kane watched as Eva's claws slowly retracted, her eyes flickering with recognition. He saw the rage that once burned within her dissipating, replaced by a deep sense of sorrow and regret. Gabriel, Magnolia, Selene, and Henry watched in awe as Eva's eyes shifted with conflicting feelings. Kane stared intensely at Eva. She growled at him, protruding her claws outwards again.

"What the hell are you talking about?!" she growled.

Kane's eyes diverted away from Eva, perusing the fallen trees that surrounded them.

"Do you know what I see when I look around this forest?" he asked.

"What?" she grunted.

"A crime against novatus potential," he answered. "In every corner of this forest are the novatus that the First Kingdom couldn't kill or enslave, so they tricked and trapped them here. This is nothing but a pen for the powerful. Seeing novatus in here sickens me to the core!"

Eva blinked slowly, engaged by Kane's words.

"And seeing you in here sickens me most of all!" he spat.

Gabriel and the others stood there silently, unsure as to a course of action. They kept to the sidelines and let Kane continue unimpeded.

"Make no mistake. Eating your mother is nothing short of a horrific crime," Kane asserted, prompting a scowl of anger and shame from Eva.

"But it *was* just a case of you going out of control. You never, *ever*, intended to hurt your mother, right?"

Eva meekly nodded; her eyes now glued to the ground. Kane took a deep breath and walked closer to her; his eyes full of compassion.

"And you never asked to be given these immense powers beyond your control, right?"

"Right…" Eva agreed, her voice cracking slightly.

"But you were, nonetheless," said Kane. "And that was *not* your fault."

Eva made eye contact with Kane, her disposition softening greatly. Slowly and surely, she morphed down out of her beast form and stood in front of him as an innocent-seeming young woman with sparkling eyes glossed by tears.

"I can't remember the last time someone spoke to me like that," Eva sighed. "Can't remember the last time someone in this damned forest treated me like anything but a rabid monster."

"Well, Eva," Kane said, his voice firm. "I think it's time you left this damned forest."

Eva's eyes brightened with hope but then lowered again with suspicion.

"Yeah right," she scoffed. "Even if I *could* leave, where the hell would I even go?"

"With us," Kane suggested. He gestured back towards Gabriel, Magnolia, Selene, and Henry, who stood further back with awkward yet warm and genuine smiles on their faces.

"Together we plan on changing everything for novatus kind," Kane told her. "And we can't do it without you."

The four nodded in corroboration with Kane. Eva looked over all of them, her eyes lingering on Kane.

"I don't know what you're talking about but if you guys genuinely know a way out of here, then I'll definitely join you with whatever you're doing," Eva said, nodding her head.

Kane smiled at Eva; the first genuine smile anyone had seen him flash in a lifetime.

"Welcome to the team!" Selene beamed at her gleefully.

Eva watched equally pleased and equally confused at the group's sudden positive reaction to her. She watched as Gabriel carefully approached her and Kane, his eyes locked on her with intensity.

"Eva…" he started. "How much do you know about the Brew of Tranquillity?"

***

Following the destruction of his castle upon the victorious battle against Enzo and the Clan of Caelestis, Grand Leader Franz Kaymore had to live elsewhere until his castle was built back up again. His new place of stay was a much smaller abode. A castle nestled within a valley surrounded by rolling hills and dense forests.

With the dozens of Vyre he had brought with him well into the First Kingdom, Nathanael Reyan approached the large wooden-door entrance to the Grand Leaders castle. As Reyan stopped by the front entrance, his soldiers behind him shifted with uncharacteristic anxiety and concern. Reyan however, remained as resolute as usual.

After a while, the door slowly opened, and Franz Kaymore came out to greet him. The Grand Leader stumbled out of the entrance, laughing, and smiling with shifting eyes. It was clear to all that he was drunk from another one of his banquets.

"Reyan!" he cheered. "It's so nice to see you aga-"

With the swiftest of strikes, Reyan cut both Franz's sentence and life short. Kaymore collapsed, bleeding profusely from a gash in his neck. The hedonistic Grand Leader writhed on the floor in deep and horrible pain. With his eyes widened he looked up to Reyan in complete and utter disbelief.

"You are a disgrace to the sanctity of the First Kingdom," he insulted the dying man. Once Kaymore was done choking on his blood, the Vyre soldiers confirmed the death, then marched off on Nathanael Reyan's lead.

***

"... you see, that's what we're trying to achieve here. We're going to travel through the kingdoms, find that lake, make that Brew of Tranquillity, and make novatus safe again!" Gabriel finished the explanation to Eva.

"I see," Eva said, a muddled look on her face. She nodded her head, processing the information overload.

"So will you join us?" asked Gabriel.

Eva glanced down at the floor. The group all waited in held breath, greatly anticipating her answer. She scratched her head and sighed.

"What we waiting for?" she said. "Let's break out here and get to the Second Kingdom."

The group's shared smiles breathed a sigh of relief toward Eva. In response, she offered a fragile, awkward smile back to the rest of the group. Her attention was drawn to Kane specifically, their eyes holding a warm gaze as they locked in on each other.

An hour later the five gathered around Henry readied the wooden cannon. Once he was done prepping the finishing touches, he turned back to the others.

"We ready?" he asked them. Collectively, they gave him a firm nod. Henry nodded back and steadied the cannon. "Right, let's do this then."

Eva transformed into her beastly lion state. She paced back and forth in preparation, her massive paws leaving deep impressions in the ground.

On Henry's cue Gabriel, Magnolia, Selene, and Kane performed their part of the plan. Lightning, earth, dark energy, and light energy shot out of their hands with a powerful combined elemental force. Henry chuckled with nervous energy as he watched the elemental concoction load up inside the cannon. The energy stored itself within the cannon, causing it to buzz and glow, shining a caramel light out of its wooden crevices. They watched in anticipation as he grabbed hold of the cannon and pointed its firing point towards the Prisoners Forests barrier above.

Henry pressed a button on the side of his cannon, igniting the firing mechanism with an explosive boom. The concentrated energy shot towards the barrier, hitting it with a deafening blow. The barrier shook and crackled under the force of the attack. The group waited in anticipation as the point of impact shook. Just as they hoped, a small tear in the barrier formed.

"Brilliant!" Magnolia cheered.

"Alright, let's go quickly before it closes back up again!" ordered Gabriel.

The five of them scaled up Lion Eva. They climbed onto her back and grasped onto her fur for dear life. She let out a roar, dragging her paws against the forest floors as she prepared to take off. It was time for her to perform her fateful jump.

Lion Eva sprang forward, her powerful legs propelling her towards the tear in the barrier. As Eva surged towards the hole, the Kin of Beasts let out a roar and extended its claws. Soon they met with the tear in the barrier just before it was about to close up again. Eva's black-tinted claws violently tore through the weakened constitution of the barrier, creating a gap large enough for them to escape.

Clinging desperately onto the fur of Eva's back, the group soared out of The Prisoners Forest. Her gigantic leap started to lose momentum as they found themselves clear from the dreaded forest of prisoners. Eva planted all paws firmly on the ground as they landed shakily with a thud and a slide. They had succeeded in safely making it to the other side.

The group turned to see now far away Prisoner's Forest from behind. They looked back at the barrier, which was now starting to repair itself. As Eva morphed back into her human form, her five new mates fell off of her back and onto the soft grass below.

The group stood in silence for a moment, catching their breath as they took in what had just happened. They shared panting chuckles and held gazes as they gathered their bearings.

"We did it," Gabriel gasped as he gazed around at the completed team - Kin of Skies, Kin of Land, Kin of Moon, Kin of Sun, Kin of Man and Kin of Beasts. They were all there. Present and accounted for.

"We did it," he repeated, smiling from ear to ear.

***

Meanwhile, further into the First Kingdom, Nathanael Reyan persisted in his efforts of 'putting people in their place,' continuing his killing spree that had started with Enzo and Franz Kaymore.

He marched through the fields of the valley, forebodingly righteous and with a fierce determination. He drew his sword as he strode forward with purpose, his eyes fixed on fleeing novatus slaves, previously owned by the late Grand Leader. His men followed closely behind him, their weapons at the ready.

The slaves scrambled across the fields, their movements desperate and frenzied. None could face Nathanael and his men, nor escape their

216

wrath. As they drew closer, Nathanael's sword flashed through the air, striking down one novatus, the energy exuding from his blade serving to take down multiple more. Reyan continued his massacring of novatus in as efficient a manner as he usually would. Only this time, with a rare smirk on his face. This time, he seemed to enjoy it.

***

Days had passed since the group had successfully retrieved their Kin of Beasts in Eva and made their escape out of the Prisoners Forest as a completed team. Now, as the evening sun began to set, they rushed to their ship by the First Kingdom shores.

Magnolia untangled the vines that concealed the vessel as the six novatus poured onto it. Exhausted by the journey, they were relieved to finally be on their way to the Second Kingdom.

Gabriel gazed out at the vast sea with hope in his eyes. "Maximilian, Aarush, Dillon. Your deaths *will not* be in vain," he said to himself quietly. "We *will* make it across all four Kingdoms. We *will* reach the lake of the brew. We *will* save our people."

*GABRIEL AND HIS COMRADES WILL CONTINUE THEIR
JOURNEY IN THE NEXT INSTALLMENT OF*

THE AUTHOR

Jason Boje is a United Kingdom-based author of fantasy, crime, sci-fi, and YA novels. He graduated with a Bachelor of Arts with Honours degree in Business Economics from Lancaster University in 2023, where he had been developing his skills in writing alongside his studies over the years. He has received numerous awards for several written works including television screenplays and online novels.

CONNECT WITH JASON VIA:

Instagram: @jasonbtgwriting

TikTok: @jasonbtgwriting

YouTube: @jasonbtg

Email: @jasontejiriboje

Printed in Great Britain
by Amazon